Martin Ross

Beggars on horseback

A riding tour in North Wales

Martin Ross

Beggars on horseback
A riding tour in North Wales

ISBN/EAN: 9783337132286

Printed in Europe, USA, Canada, Australia, Japan

Cover: Foto ©Andreas Hilbeck / pixelio.de

More available books at **www.hansebooks.com**

BEGGARS ON HORSEBACK

A RIDING TOUR IN NORTH WALES

BY

MARTIN ROSS

AND

E. Œ. SOMERVILLE

AUTHORS OF 'AN IRISH COUSIN,' 'THROUGH CONNEMARA,'
'THE REAL CHARLOTTE,' ETC. ETC.

*WITH NUMEROUS ILLUSTRATIONS
BY E. Œ. SOMERVILLE*

WILLIAM BLACKWOOD AND SONS
EDINBURGH AND LONDON
MDCCCXCV

ILLUSTRATIONS.

BEGGARS ON HORSEBACK.

CHAPTER I.

"WELL, I'm not exactly sure," said the ironmonger, gazing out into the glaring street through a doorway festooned with tin mugs and gridirons, "but I think it was the gentleman as played the kettle-drum that rode him." His eyes seemed to follow some half-remembered pageant, though outwardly they rested on the languid salutations of the saddler's dog and the hotel collie on the opposite pavement.

Miss O'Flannigan, who looked and was too hot for conversation, remained impassive where she sat, on the top of an "Empress" cottage stove, with her gaze fixed on the zinc pails that hung like Chinese lanterns from the ceiling.

A

"Unfortunately we shall not take a kettle-drum," I replied, hesitatingly.

"Well, no, of course," admitted the ironmonger; "but I assure you that a pony that's bin in the yeomanry band won't be partikler as to traction-engines or sech. You ladies could play any instrument when ridin' 'im."

Miss O'Flannigan laughed sardonically from the "Empress" stove, and Mr Griffiths' attitude of mild bewilderment changed to wounded dignity.

"Perhaps Mr Williams, the chemist, could oblige you with sech animals as you require," he said, with the stiffness of one of his own swing-door hinges; "but there isn't sech a cob in Welshpool as what my cob is."

We temporised with Mr Griffiths and proceeded to the chemist's, noticing as we did so a determination of the inhabitants of Welshpool to their shop doors, while the loafers round the stone pedestal of the gas lamp that seems to form the focus of Welshpool life, turned to look after us like sunflowers to the sun. Further away than ever went

the memory of the thud of 'bus-horses' feet on
wood pavement, the hot glitter of harness and
livery buttons at Hyde Park Corner, the pre-
carious dive across Piccadilly, and all the other
environments of yesterday. The heat of noon
lay here like a spell on the street, and Welshpool,
for the most part, sat in its shady back parlours
in comfortable lethargy.

Like the other shops, Mr Williams, the chemist's, was cool and empty, with the air of a
place where it is always dinner-hour hanging
drowsily over it. Indeed, the pimpled cheek of
the apprentice — why are pimples the common
wear of chemists' assistants? — was still inflated
by a mouthful when he made his appearance,
and a sound as of dumpling impeded the voice
in which he told us that Mr Williams had a
pony, and that the mistress would speak to us
herself.

"Mr Williams was away," explained Mrs
Williams, "drawing teeth and measuring for
new ones; and y'know what a job that is," she

concluded, examining Miss O'Flannigan's smile

She sat on the top of an " Empress" cottage stove.

with the eye of a connoisseur.   Miss O'Flannigan
relapsed somewhat abruptly into gloom.

"I have a pair of real little beauties," went on

The obliging ironmonger.

the chemist's wife, beaming at us between minarets
of Eno's Fruit Salt and Mellin's Food, "just the

thing for London work. I'll have them round
at the hotel for you in ten minutes."

We were conscious of social shrinkage as the
work for which we required the ponies was explained ; a fortnight's road work in Wales, with
the proviso that the animals would have to carry
packs—"large packs," added Miss O'Flannigan—
held a suggestion of bagmen, not to say tinkers.
But Mrs Williams' stable sank unhesitatingly to
the level of our needs.   She had yet another
pony, three years old, thirteen hands high, steady,
"and bin ridden with the Yeomanry," she ended,
reassuringly.

From the eye that Miss O'Flannigan cast upon
me I knew that her mind was, like mine, occupied
with a vision of the Yeomanry mounted, like
cyclists, on "dwarf-safeties," and we ventured to
ask whether the St Bernard, whose eyes gleamed
from the dark corner of the shop where he lay,
pantingly protruding a tongue like a giant slice
of ham, had been ridden during the training.
The jest had a high success, and a suetty giggle

from somewhere near the open door of the parlour apprised us that this gem of Irish humour
was not lost on the apprentice.

Before we returned to the hotel several things
had been accomplished. We were possessors of
the chemist's pony for a fortnight; we had bak-
ingly retraced our steps to the ironmonger, and
by dint of remaining immutable on the top of
the cottage stove, had made a like bargain with
him; and we had interested Welshpool more
whole-souledly than any event since the election
and the last circus. Coolness and peace awaited
us at the Royal Oak Inn, with its thick walls and
polished floors, and its associations of the old
coaching days, wonderfully striking to an Irish
eye, accustomed to connect antiquity with dirt
and dilapidation. We have nothing hale and
honourable like these hostelries, with their centuries of landlord ancestry: we have the modern
hotel after its kind, and also the unspeakable pot-
house, with creeping things after their kind; but
antiquity, if such there be, is a poor, musty

ghost, lingering among broken furniture and pot-
sherds, to sadden the eyes of such as can dis-
cern it.

Ireland seemed a long way off, while we lunched
largely and languidly on fruit and cream, and
wondered how we were going to ride through four
counties in heat of this kind. A sense of inadequacy grew upon us like a slight indigestion, or,
perhaps, it came to us in that guise, and the fussy
clatter of ponies' hoofs in the yard below had a ring
in it of the inexorable. Miss O'Flannigan sharp-
ened a pencil and began to make notes, evidently
to restore her moral tone,—notes about Welshpool,
she said, antiquities, and such things ; but as subsequently these proved to consist of the entry,
"Saturday, June 10, 'Black and White,' lunch,
Academy, headache, tea, tried on, &c.," with a
bulbous profile of the ironmonger, her method of
working back to ancient history must have been
mystic and gradual.

While we thus sat dubious of ourselves and
all things, expecting to hear that the chemist and

the ironmonger had alike thought better of it, there
was a shuffling of many feet in the hall, and the
door opened to its widest to admit an immense
old lady, advancing with the solemnity of a hearse,
while two daughters of some fifty-five or sixty
hard-won years moved beside her like pall-bearers,
supporting each a weighty elbow on their lean
arms. A third daughter walked behind, carrying
a white dog of the Spitz breed. As a foundation-
stone sinks to its resting-place, so, and with a like
deliberation, was the old lady lowered into the
largest and, indeed, the only possible chair; one
daughter shut the window, another rang the bell,
and a meal of fried beef-steak, onions, and bottled
stout was ordered. The temperature of the room
seemed perceptibly to rise, and Miss O'Flannigan
and I communed by glances as to whether we
had energy to get up and go away.

"Eh! it's warm, vera warm," said the old lady,
addressing the company in general, but ceaselessly
examining Miss O'Flannigan and me with eyes as
blue and bright as those of any heroine of inex-

pensive fiction ; "it mak's a body p'spire **vera free,**
that it dew. But ye dew enjoy it——"

She spoke with **a** Yorkshire accent as broad **as**
the foot which, in its cloth shoe and white stock-
ing, was handsomely displayed below her **skirt**
hem—and we apologise for probable mistakes in
the reproduction by an Irish hand of that **sturdy,**
grumbling drawl.

"Ah'm come all **the** way oop fra' Yorkshire **for**
a too-er," **she went on ;** "t' yoong folks like **a**
change," she indicated her grey-haired attendants,
"but Wales is a bit dool **when ye** come out **for**
a holiday. Eh, Scarbro's the gay, bonny **place !**
Eh, but **ye** miss a **treat if** ye don't see Scarbro!"

She held us with **her** glittering eye, and **the**
eulogy of Scarborough proceeded with the burr
of a noontide **bee,** by promenades, hotels, family
histories of friends who kept lodgings **in the best**
terraces, and many other highways and byways ;
while the three daughters and the white dog **sat**
and filled in **the mesmeric** effect, immovable as
scenery. **A message** that the ponies **were** in **the**

yard came at last to our relief, like good news
from a far country, and with the activity of a
hunting morning we made our exit in the wake
of the waitress, who, at the Royal Oak, as at
many other Welsh inns, has worthily replaced
the waiter and the cheerless glory of his evening suit. The needed fillip had been given ; the
present moment, with its release and its ponies,
sparkled suddenly, and that Wales which the old
Yorkshire woman found so "dool" by comparison
with Scarborough, lay awaiting us in restored
glamour.

The large, clean yard, with its respectable coaching and fox-hunting associations, was acquiring a
new experience. The loafers had detached themselves from the lamp-post, the tide of commerce
had flowed from the shops to stand round the
stable doors, and discuss in the guttural, shrewish
Welsh tongue what manner of she-yeomanry they
might be who thus requisitioned Welshpool ponies
for their own undivulged purposes. There was a
dead silence as we came forth, hobbling and

waddling in our fettering safety habit-skirts — a
silence, as we hope, of admiration, but we have
not inquired into it.   The ponies were there—a
bay of a little over fourteen hands, a chestnut dun
of a hand smaller, both ill - fitted by their big
saddles, both possessed of a generous contour
that told of long summer days of revelling in
the young grass, and summer nights of serious
gobbling of it when the flies were asleep.   Mr
Williams the chemist, and Mr Griffiths the ironmonger, stood at their heads, and began a species
of funeral oration upon their virtues, and upon the
pangs of parting from them ; while an attendant,
with his knee against the side of the bay, and his
head buried under the flap of the saddle, exerted
what strength was in him to overcome the pangs
of meeting exhibited by the girths and their
buckles : nothing remained for us except to mount,
and to trust that we should be spared disaster in
the eyes of Welshpool.

Miss O'Flannigan asked the name of the bay
pony, and having ascertained that it was Tom, com-

manded that he should be brought to the mount-
ing-block. Tom, a three-year-old of precocious
gravity, erstwhile bearer of the kettle-drum and
possessed of the serious good looks of one of Mrs
Sherwood's curates, reluctantly approached the
hoary limestone block, with a horrified eye fixed
on Miss O'Flannigan as she awaited him in her
safety skirt. Persuasion failed to bring him within
three yards of a garment which, as he doubtless
expressed it, would have made Mrs Sherwood turn
in her grave; and Miss O'Flannigan was finally
pitched on to his back from an indefinite spot
near the stable door, whither, with one foot in the
stirrup, she had hopped in pursuit of her steed. It
was damping to find that the name of the chemist's
pony was Tommy, but we felt sure that in the first
few minutes of our first journey we should think
of something clever with which to re-christen
both. We subsequently spent several hours of
several journeys in this endeavour, but their bap-
tismal names have not as yet been improved on.

"He iss a little unused to the town, marm," said

the chemist's stable-boy, as Tommy submitted
with unexpected calm to the infliction of my
weight; "but he iss goot—yes, indeed!"

"He iss a little unused to the town, marm."

The next moment I was pursuing Miss O'Flannigan up the street like the conventional pattern
of a flash of lightning. Happily, the houses, carts,
barrels, and other objects possessed of terrors for

Tommy alternated on either side with tolerable
regularity, so that one shy acted as a corrective
to the last; but these advantages were denied
to Miss O'Flannigan. Her Tom fled along before
me, cantering with the fore and trotting widely
with the hind legs, and making startling attempts
to turn in at unexpected side entrances—attempts
that were only frustrated by serious effort on the
part of his rider.

It was somewhere during this rush through
Welshpool and its environs, while the saddles rolled
and our faces blazed, that we were conscious of
passing a building like a Methodist chapel, from
which came men's and women's voices, singing in
harmony. It was only a moment's hearing, but
it lived, ringing and resonant, in our ears, and is
notable still to us as our first experience of Welsh
voices. When, at sunset, we returned dishevelled
and hairpinless, but masters of the situation, Miss
O'Flannigan had remembered several quotations
from the poets to express the effect of these keen,
strong voices flung out into the sleepy afternoon.

I, regarding the heat-stained coats of the Tommies
and Miss O'Flannigan's back-hair, could remember
nothing except the conversation of two men at
a race meeting in Galway—

"Did ye see them skelping round by Glan
corner?"

"I did not, faith."

"Then ye seen nothing."

CHAPTER II.

THERE are no suburbs to Welshpool. Practical, like its countrywomen, it does not trail a modish skirt across the meadows; the woods and hedge-rows run down to it, but it will not change its working-dress and come up from its hollow to be idle with them. Of this, indeed, we were not dis-posed to complain, when at some three of the clock on the next afternoon we started on the first stage of our journey. We had received, in the act of departure, an amount of interest and attention that would have satiated, not to say embarrassed, a sandwich-man—from the congre-gated friends of the chemist and ironmonger, from the old Yorkshire woman (framed like a Holbein behind the glass of a firmly closed window), from

B

the exponents of fashion in baggy breeches and slim gaiters who habitually "practised at the bar" of the hotel, from the carriage of an unknown magnate, and from the pit and gallery section which had early possessed itself of the best places on the central lamp-post. The subtler observation of villa residences was at least spared us, the vulture eye of the tradesman's widow behind the lace curtain, the scorn of the offspring of the dentist or the auctioneer.

Powys Castle and its woods towered aloof in a shimmer of heat, as unaware of town and tourist as the cattle within its gates. The grey houses of the town became smaller and older looking; cats sat on the doorstep and mused on the deceitfulness of things, overawing the languid dogs in the eternal supremacy of mind over matter; and the flame of sunshine blazed tangibly round us and all things. Our last impression of Welshpool is of its oldest house, a black-beamed cottage, lolling and bulging, crooked and bowed in every line; impossible as to perspective, but strong and

stable beyond all houses in the town—so the town
says. Then the hedgerows, and the white road
stretching westward into the unknown. Elder-
bushes, with their creamy discs; dog-roses of every
shade of pink gazing at us with soft innumerable
faces; honeysuckle in thickets; perfumes lonely
and delicate, perfumes blended and intoxicating.
The thought of them takes the pen from the paper
in indolent remembrance of that first ride between
the Montgomery hedgerows, while yet the horse-
flies had not discovered us, and while the hold-alls
lay trim and deceptive in the straps that bound
them to the saddles.

The mention of the hold-alls disperses like an
east wind all ideas of the indolent and the picturesque. Briefly they may be described as was a
kitchen-maid in a Galway household by an en-
raged fellow-servant—"She's able to put any one
that'd be with her into a decay." We had spent
the morning in packing them, in repacking them,
in acrid argument as to whether Miss O'Flannigan's painting-box (apparently made of lead and

filled with stones) would fit in my hold-all with the
teapot, tin kettle, india-rubber bath, shooting-boots,
drugs, and other angular things which had been
already bestowed in it; in punching fresh holes
in the straps, in going to the saddler to have more
"dees" put on the off-sides of the saddles, and
finally in a harrowing parting with our portmanteaus, which, labelled "Dolgelly, per goods train,"
had been delivered to the hand of the boots. It
was the burning of the ships; and while the smart,
tightly-belted hold-alls were hoisted like plethoric
grooms to their saddles, we looked back to the
portmanteaus, and said, with a hope no larger
than Brutus had, "If we do meet again, we'll smile
indeed."

For about two miles we crawled at a walk in the
heat,—the drab Tommy niggling, shuffling, and
plodding; the bay Tom "dishing," crossing his
legs, and stumbling, but both absolutely laid out
for goodness. Lulled to a false security, we
ambled thus up and down the slopes, and prosed
a little to each other about the scenery: plump,

Packing the "hold-alls."

knobby hills, such as one would cut out of dough
with a tumbler, with strips of wood straddling over
them ; rich valleys with their sides padded with
dark-green trees, all complete and devoid of relation to each other, but all similar, like a picture-
gallery full of replicas of the same landscape.
This, we said, was not the kind of thing we had
come to Wales to see.

A shaded stretch of road tempted us at length
to urge the Tommies to their own wild trot, and
to its vagaries we and the hold-alls rose and fell,
bumped and joggled with what grace we might.
Roadside heaps of stones, that had till now been
merely matter for composed inquiry to the
Tommies, became at this pace fraught with all
supernatural powers and malign intents, and we
cannoned violently and often, as Tom swerved,
wild-eyed, from one of these objects of terror,
or as Tommy, the ignoble, turned with incredible
swiftness and endeavoured to flee home to the
chemist. We persevered to the top of a steep
descent, where the white dusty road fell away

from our feet, and there slackened as there came
into view a cart drawn by four giant horses with
solemn bowed heads and huge legs that gave
them the effect of wearing sailor's trousers, tight
at the knee and full at the ankle. The trunk of
a great elm lay on the cart, a "vibrating star,"
as George Eliot has described the prone advance
of such another tree, and on top of it sat a man
in a blue linen coat, looking as unimportant as
a squirrel in relation to the mammoth creatures
who were accepting his authority. We looked
at him with respect as the quivering bole of the
elm-tree drew slowly level with us, but he regarded
us not at all. His gaze was fixed on my hold-all,
from whose gaping mouth, as we suddenly became
aware, a sponge-bag and the spout of the tea-kettle
were protruding.

"Hoy!" said the carter, pointing with his
brass-ringed whip at something on the road
behind us.

It was Miss O'Flannigan's india-rubber cup, a
noisome vessel from which she indifferently partook

of tea, bovril, and claret. We dismounted, and the
saddles, released from the compensating balance of
the weight that experience had already taught us
to bring to bear on the stirrups, obeyed instantly
the four-stone drag of each hold-all, and began to
turn very slowly and steadily to the off-side. We
collected the cup and some other scattered valu-
ables, and then, while the flies closed in round us,
we began the long strife with straps and buckles.
The Tommies sidled, stamped, and snapped un-
governably ; while the flies devoured us and them
impartially, the girths were dragged to their last
holes, the hold-alls repacked and strapped on
again, and the reign of suffering that ceased not
till our journey's end was fairly inaugurated.

Cannoffice was our destination, Llanfair was to
be our stopping-place for tea. I almost hesitate
to mention that Llanfair is but seven miles from
Welshpool ; but it is, perhaps, better to state at
once that we, and, still more, the Tommies, were
above the vulgarities of record-breaking, unless,
indeed, we can lay claim to our daily journeys

being the shortest hitherto performed by any Welsh tourist. It must have been five o'clock when we rode down the stony hill beside the no less dry and stony river-bed, where at any time, except in this rainless year, the water must swirl pleasantly below the grey village of Llanfair. Welsh villages are composed of nearly equal parts of inns and chapels, so that such names as " The Cross Foxes," "Rehoboth," "The Goat," "The Grapes," "Addoldy," "Salem," and "Bethesda," greet the traveller in startling succession. We crossed the humpbacked bridge, above the fevered bed of the river, where the children sat and played at giving parties with many long drowned crockeries, and we rode the length of the little street and selected the last of the inns that clung to its steep sides.

It was the glimpse of oak settles and panels, and gleams of old brass and copper, that we saw through the open door of the Wynnstay Arms that turned the scale, already tilted by the vision of a fat ostler boy with gold earrings, who grinned

from the stable opposite. That he spoke English
about as well as a French porter at Calais was
subsequently a drawback, when it came to words
like surcingle and hold-all, and the beautiful

The fat ostler boy.

kitchen with the tiled floor and the high settles
(and we are compelled to add, the spittoons) was
not permitted to us. For us was reserved the
fusty decorum of an upper parlour, obviously

consecrate to domestic ceremonies,—funeral cards
and the plaster ornament of a wedding - cake
formed the chimney ornaments,—to the rare female
visitor, and to a vow that the windows should not
be opened. We cannot, however, look back otherwise than with affection to the tea which presently
came to us, to the cream and the bread-and-butter,
and to the fact that it was the first and last "plain
tea" which Wales supplied us with at sixpence
each.

The journey to Cannoffice was resumed with reluctance on our part and on the part of the Tommies, who were beginning to think that the thing
was getting past a joke and looked horribly like
business. Our best sympathies were given to them
as we fought our way along the remainder of
that afternoon's sixteen miles, decimating use-
lessly the hungry host of horse-flies that every
hedge recruited, flying from them at a ludicrous
full gallop, waving them back with branches of
trees ; perhaps it would be truer to say that the
Tommies had our second-best sympathies. The

noblest compassion of our hearts was lavished
on ourselves. The Tommies certainly played
their part in the strife with ingenuity that, in
some degree, made up for the inadequacy of
their pigmy tails. They kicked flies off their
stomachs and shoulders as artlessly and easily
as dogs; they bit their legs down to the pastern;
they rubbed themselves against the delicious
angularities of the hold-alls; they buried their
faces in our habits in a way that would have
been maddening, if it had not appealed so tor-
turingly to our pity.

It was eight o'clock before we reached Cannoffice, and the brilliant sky of summer had lost
but little of its radiancy. We and the Tommies
had perceptibly lost ours, but still the thing was
done. We had passed from among the lumpy
green hills, and had, by slow ascent, reached
more open country, which had a tendency and
a meaning in its strong, large, upward curve.
Already the faint ridge of the mountains was
on the horizon, and the balm of the uplands was

in the air.   The old Cannoffice Inn looked pleasantly at us out
of its ivied win-
dows and
low porch;
we took it
for the vic-
arage till
we saw up-
on it the

The first flies.

mystic sign of the winged wheel which marks

the approval of the cyclist club. In the evening, when we wandered between the dense beech and yew hedges of the garden, or sat in a dark arbour and heard the cattle cropping the dewy grass, the ineffable pastoralities of the place made themselves felt. Children and dogs were playing noisily on a hill opposite; out in the unseen hamlet behind a grove of pine-trees there was now and then a distant snatch of voices singing in harmony; and garden perfumes, cooled in night air, spoke of peace and of a hundred sleeping roses. We forgot that our legs were stiffening into acute angles, that our foreheads had been phrenologically remodelled by horse-fly bites, and that our house-shoes were circling round Wales in a luggage-train. And that, I think, was how I caught one of my very finest colds in my head.

CHAPTER III.

NEXT morning Miss O'Flannigan went out sketching. The casual reader may skim this information
permissively, as a harmless, picturesque thing, very
proper for young ladies; but to the companion
of· Miss O'Flannigan's travels it has other aspects.
For example, the aspect of Miss O'Flannigan herself, as she sat on a paling with her feet tucked
up, her hat tilted over a scarlet face, and her teeth
clenched on a spare paint-brush; or mine, as I
leaned on the rail of a footbridge over against
her, in the furnace heat of the sun, with what
negligence remains to the model who has stiffened
for twenty minutes in the attitude so lightly and
luxuriously undertaken. It must be admitted,
however, that the cold caught the night before

*Next morning Miss O'Flannigan
went out sketching.*

was, in that unrelenting blaze, slowly baked away.
Probably the children who sat along the banks
of the stream and discussed us in Welsh saw it
rise like a mist and melt into the blue: Miss
O'Flannigan did not see it, but when painting
she sees nothing but values. Ordinary humanity
does not see values any more than fairies, but
Miss O'Flannigan and other artists do.

It was afternoon when we forsook the simplici-
ties of Cannoffice, and went forth to the unknown
and the unpronounceable. Five minutes' stroll
will exploit the place, with its half-dozen ancient
cottages, its "Zion," and its post-office, where
English is a difficulty, and the forwarding of a
letter to a given address a problem too deep to
be grappled with. But Cannoffice does not seem
greatly to care whether its visitors stay minutes
or months. Incorruptibly sylvan and indomitably
Welsh, it shakes off the dust of each tourist
season, and returns to its solitary and sufficing
ways of life, and there are moments when one
could wish to return with it.

Up into the west we went, along a road hilly
and pastoral, lonely and hot. After some miles
of it we dived into a fir-grove and emerged into
a region of a strangely different sort. Connemara
it might have been—the back of Connemara by the
Erriff river—such and of such a greenness were
the hills; so amongst them, along the marshy
level, ran the unfenced road. Not a tree broke
the tender barrenness of the outlines: big and
mild, with the magnanimous curves of the brows
of an elephant, the hills stood clothed in the sweet
short grass; and among their hollows grazed sheep
and black cattle, whose smallness may have been
native, or may have been a deception of that
great feeding-ground. We halted there in breezy
silences where no horse-fly inhabited, and had an
afternoon tea of patriarchal frugality,—a bunch
of raisins and a crust of bread cut with Miss
O'Flannigan's pocket-knife, which had last been
used for scraping out a tin of soft-soap.

The country closed in round us as we journeyed.
Ravines clove the hills, woods ran hardily on the

steeps, and stone walls replaced the hedges. The road rose to higher levels, winding parapeted above the ravines, and we began to meet people again—people of a politeness incredible, almost unnerving, to those whose belief in their own appearance has been sapped by various adversities, especially the insecurity of hairpins. Voices were on the hillsides, and once from the bottom of a ravine came up most freshly the lilt of a woman's song. The words were Welsh, the tune unknown, but all clean and homely romance was borne on the notes of that careless, yet half-melancholy, peasant voice.

Following on this the rattle of a mowing-machine grated upon the farthest edge of silence, and going on towards it we came on an inn, the only one boasted of by the village of Mallwydd.

Thrice we rode to and fro before that humble hostelry, and, but for a weird, pig-styish smell which pervaded the village, had committed ourselves to it. We escaped from the expectant

landlady, and applied the Tommies to the mile
that remained between us and Dinas Mowddy—
having, at all events, discovered that Maäthlooith
and Deenas Mawthy were approximately the pro-
nunciations for the two places. After a quarter
of an hour we seemed nearer to nothing except
a slate-quarry, and we addressed ourselves to a
passer-by of majestic respectability on the subject
of the Griffith Arms Hotel. This person informed
us, with the utmost difficulty and with much pan-
tomime, that " the hotel wass inside—yess indeed,"
but beyond this his English did not carry him.
In that language he did not know his right hand
from his left, and graphic semaphoring on Miss
O'Flannigan's part did not seem to convey anything to his mind,— made him indeed hasten
onwards, as one who finds he is entertaining a
lunatic unawares.

As a matter of history, the Griffith Arms is
inside nothing ; it stands bare and square by the
roadside, without so much as a garden paling
before it. But there is a great deal outside it.

A splendid hill, covered to the summit with blue-green pine-trees, looms up in front of it; behind is a long valley, pierced through the heart by a flashing mountain-stream; all round are more hills topped with yet more pine-woods; a snow-peak and a châlet would have made it Switzerland; and doubtless, in these days of enterprise and Earl's Court, the thing could be arranged.

The hotel seemed to be well stocked with visitors. We had believed ourselves to be before the season, and yet through the shrubs of a garden at the end of the house we saw several ladies in bright-coloured blouses, sitting on garden seats and tending children of all ages, a most edifying and domestic spectacle; and I began to be sorry for Miss O'Flannigan, who had refused to take advice and a walking skirt, and would have to come down to dinner in her habit. Within was a strange emptiness—a large uninhabited coffee-room, an absence of *table d'hôte*, and an assiduous interest on the part of the landladies, of whom there seemed to be several. Apparently the vir-

tuous band of mother tourists fed early with their
progeny, for we dined alone. It seemed a little
unusual when presently, from the windows of the
coffee-room, we saw the chambermaid (a tall and
handsome lady, with manners that quelled any
suggestion of familiarity from us) go forth to the
pleasure-ground, and, having seated herself, pro-
ceed to tell a convulsingly funny story to the
tourists. We should have liked to have heard
it, but could catch nothing except an inquiry
shrieked by an auditor through the drowning
laughter, "Did 'e say 'Ma little duck'?" which
awakened a persecuting curiosity while it deepened the mystery.

We examined the Visitors' Book. No trace of
the party was in it, unless it was indirectly hinted
at by a cyclist, who, with that happy vein of
humour and inventiveness of spelling with which
Visitors' Books are so replete, dilated on the
"gossopping gardens" of the hotel. Many things
were strange about the Griffith Arms. It was
full of unseen presences, of suggestions of an

inner life not subordinate to hotel routine, and we
roamed solitary in their midst. The big, panelled
bath-room, where before dinner I simmered off
the fatigues of the ride, had the stale discouraged
air of a room that has been left severely to itself.
Its breath was heavy with suggestions of the
wearing apparel that lined its shelves and hung
in decaying grandeur on pegs on the door, and
in the bath itself lay a pair of baby's boots, thick,
knitted ones, evidently forgotten there since winter.
Miss O'Flannigan's wardrobe contained an interesting selection of walking-sticks, fishing-tackle, razors,
ties of the class known as "Jemima," and finally,
in a separate compartment, innumerable pairs of
socks. They belonged to Mr Willy Griffith, the
chambermaid explained, with the manner of one
who disarms all objections in advance. He stayed
at the hotel very often for fishing. She made
the same reply when I commented, not unkindly,
on the presence of several dozen pairs of socks
and six well-greased fishing-boots in my chest
of drawers. We did not venture to argue the

matter, though it compelled us to distribute the contents of the hold-alls upon the floor.

Early next morning the house rang with the shrieks that accompanied the toilet of many children; and though the coffee-room was at breakfast-time as desolate as ever, the garden presently became filled to a state of *crèche*-like repletion, and Miss O'Flannigan and I wandered forth in search of a resting-place less fraught with domesticity. We made for the pine-clothed flanks of Moel Dinas, but the heat was terrific— the pine-trees were too young to keep it out, though they were old enough to hide the view; the flies were beyond belief, and the hot perfume from the trees became at last intolerable. We crept back to the hotel and lay about in the shadeless coffee-room, and it was afternoon before we discovered .coolness by going down to the river and sitting on damp rocks in a draught under an arch of the new bridge, with the old one picturesquely visible in the background, while the children, the mothers, and the chambermaid

"A youth of shop-walker beauty, in the guise of a fisherman."

held high carnival in the garden above. It was
here, probably, that Mr Willy Griffith cast his flies
when in residence at the Griffith Arms ; and Miss
O'Flannigan absently added the figure of a youth

"We caught a glimpse of a grey beard and a Tyrolean hat."

of shop-walker beauty, in the guise of a fisherman,
to the series of enervated scribbles which marked
her sketch-book's progress through that long hot
Sunday. She was descending to the addition of

an eyeglass and a cigarette, when a pebble
dropped into the water beside us. As we looked
up to the parapet of the bridge, another pebble
was dropped, and there was an eldritch falsetto
laugh. We caught one difficult glimpse of a grey
beard and a Tyrolean hat, a running footstep
resounded above, and then silence. It seemed
time for evening church, and we retired.

CHAPTER IV.

A DARK-FACED Kelt in a blue suit was reading the First Lesson as we made our entry. Bearing in mind Miss O'Flannigan's riding-habit, it required nerve to present ourselves to the Church of Mallwydd at this shelterless stage of the service, but the congregation appeared to be inured to tourists. They scarcely ceased in their attention to the reader, and to his serious and careful rendering of the Lesson in his native tongue. "Darkling we listened" until the twice repeated "Samooel, Samooel," suddenly flung out

from the dark stream of Welsh, apprised us that
it was the call of Samuel and the humiliation of
Eli with which his strong brows rose or bent in
sympathy.

Behind the reader was a glimpse of a surpliced
arm, and a pale and languid hand supporting a
grey head with the air of melancholy befitting a
pastor of the Church of Wales at the present
crisis. The thought of coming disaster was in-
separable from him and the venerable little church,
while the service progressed through prayers and
hymns with a fervour worthy of dissent ; and
when the grey head and the sad face were above
us in the pulpit, and the text, " The violent take it
by force," was given out in Welsh and English,
it was easy to imagine the drift of the sermon
that followed, spoken, or rather sung, as the
Welsh manner is, in the preacher's native tongue.
With the monotony of a mountain wind, with
the swinging cadence of a belfry, the minor
periods rose and died. It might have been the
sombre prophesying of a Druid, chanted beneath

the oaks in days prior to Gregorians; it seemed
to have in it echoes from ages of forgotten per-
secution, to be passionate with the protest of a
threatened faith. The modern respectability of
the congregation was amazingly out of keeping
with it, but many of the listening faces were
keen with unmistakable response. We recognised
in different parts of the church some of the deni-
zens of the Griffith Arms with their offspring—
being, in fact, privileged to sit behind certain of
the latter, and to mark the methods by which
they wiled away the duration of the state prayers
and other unbearable disciplines. It was something of a shock to discover the chambermaid
seated in amity and a chancel pew beside a
venerable gentleman whose grey beard had an
unstudied luxuriance about it that recalled the
pebble-thrower at the bridge. He stared at us
with an excitement that seemed to deepen into
ferocity, and once, during the prayers, I am almost certain that I saw him—after a wary glance
at the chambermaid — thrust out his tongue,

D

apparently at us. What had he to do with the
chambermaid, and why did he object to us?
These things were hid from us.

Let no one ask from these historians the facts
about the Behemoth skull and the Leviathan
backbone which are disposed in the timbered
arch above the porch-door of the church. There
are theories and there are legends, all equally
improbable, so we were informed by the grey-
haired vicar, with a classic and tolerant weariness
which may well have been caused by the heat,
or the Suspensory Bill, or the fact that Miss
O'Flannigan was perhaps the five thousandth
tourist by whom he had been asked the same
question.

That night the order went forth for a half-past
six o'clock breakfast. If the heat was tropical,
so should be our manner of life, and the ride
over the mountains to Dolgelly should be in the
dewy cool of the morning. Nothing could be
more idyllic. This quality, however, was not so
prominent next morning, when at 6.15 A.M. Miss

"Miss O'Flannigan's hair came down."

O'Flannigan ranged forth through the sleeping
house to call the chambermaid, or when at 7.15
the underdone poached eggs and the chill phantom
of yesterday's coffee were achieved by the cook
in some favourable interval of her toilet. Nor,
by the time that we had arranged ourselves upon
the Tommies, was the coolness so striking as we
could have wished, except in the representative
of the landladies, with whom we had had occasion
to discuss the bill. This matter caused an awk-
wardness in our usually effective farewells — so
much so that we felt constrained to start at full
gallop, and to keep up the pace till we believed
ourselves out of sight of the group at the hotel
door. The Tommies shied as though before that
hour they had never looked on the things of
earth, and the firry flank of the Moel Dinas had
not intervened when Miss O'Flannigan's hair came
down and the strap of my hold-all had burst.
A more determined effort than usual on Tommy's
part to go home placed me for a moment facing
the Griffith Arms,—a glimpse worth gathering, dis-

covering as it did the fact that the unexplained
guests of the hotel, in varied and immature cos-
tumes, were exulting at every upper window, and
that from the window of the apartment that had
so recently been ours—the room that we had been
told belonged to Mr Willy Griffith—waved the
white beard of the old man of the bridge and the
church.   Was he Mr Willy Griffith ?

We leave the problem, together with the *raison
d'être* of the female tourists, to be dealt with by
future visitors to the Griffith Arms, of whose
company we are not likely to be.

It is not necessary to enter into details of the
half-hour that followed. Let it be understood
that I mended my strap with my pocket-handkerchief, that Miss O'Flannigan did her hair with
three surviving hairpins, and that we received
all possible assistance from the horse-flies.

The midsummer sun in the heart of the Welsh
mountains is bad to beat. It was blazing when
we began the long ascent from the valley as
though it had been at it all night—as, indeed, I

suppose it had, somewhere or other — and until
that early morning ride we cannot be said to have
properly known what the word heat might mean.
The pine-clad hills were storehouses of it, and
gave it forth, fragrantly, after their kind, but
suffocatingly. We had no umbrellas, no lessening
of our apparel was possible ; we were pitiable beyond all parties of pleasure. In stupor we emerged
from the wooded country, and followed the long
beckonings of a mountain-road, a lonely streak
that climbed and climbed on the back of a green,
tremendous hill. Other hills, sons of Anak, stood
all about, with that same lucent, beryl greenness
spread in smooth simplicity on their sweeping
contours. Grey cottages lying far below and far
apart in the great hollows, were as specks no
larger than sheep. The sheep themselves had
abandoned all attempt at grazing, and had essayed
to hide from the sun in the cracks and crannies of
the more broken ground at the top of the pass.
From these they looked forth on us, dignified as
Dons in their stalls at Oxford, but ready at an

instant's warning to exhibit "a passion and ecstasy
of flight" not common in the Don.   The hillsides
were alive with their solemn faces ; they were the
only living things we saw, except two old men
mending the road as an Irishman mends his house,
with the nearest promiscuous stone and a clod of
earth.

When it came to the descent of the mountain,
we resolved to be merciful and lead the Tommies—
a praiseworthy benevolence, but one not valued by
Tom as it should have been.   With stiff forelegs
and resentful eye, he was dragged by Miss O'Flannigan down the immeasurable lengths of steep
road, protesting in every hair against a mode of
progress that was not, to his conservative mind,
justified by precedent.   Moreover, being sensitive
to what was *outré* in appearance, he may have
taken exception to the puggaree made by Miss
O'Flannigan out of bracken and a painting rag ;
but as, to our certain knowledge, he would have
hungrily eaten either if left alone with it, we cannot but regard this as an affectation.

He was dragged by Miss O'Flannigan down the immeasurable lengths of steep road.

We neared again the freely - wooded valley
scenery of which Wales keeps such store. Cader
Idris was suddenly on our left, bare and fierce and
coarsely magnificent : very different from our first
far-away glimpse of it as a pale ethereal creature
of the horizon — a fit companion for the most
heavenly clouds of sunset. It meant that Dolgelly was near, but we began to doubt that we
should ever reach Dolgelly. We galloped in
desperation through the blinding heat ; we recovered ourselves in the patches of shade. Our
heads swam, our throats were as dry as the tra-
ditional lime-burner's wig, and we thought, with
a kind of passion, of Irish south-westerly gales
bursting in floods of rain.

We drew rein at a shady roadside spring, at
whose thin trickle a gipsy woman was filling an
earthenware jug. Here should the Tommies drink
their fill, while perchance a sketch was made of
the tilt of the gipsy waggon, half hidden in trees
a little back off the road. But the Tommies had
other views. Panic-struck, they recoiled from that

innocent trickle of water as from a thing bewitched ;
they whirled, trembled, snorted, and finally abandoned themselves to a *sauve-qui-peut* flight in the
direction of Dolgelly.

During the last half-hour the road grew more
and more civilised ; the "Cross Foxes" uplifted
its popular sign by the roadside, villas were frequent, the scenery was charming, but we cared for
none of these things. All we desired was a cool
death—"something lingering," with icebergs in it.
We rode into the grey town of Dolgelly at 10.30
o'clock, having started at six, and accomplished
twelve miles. It was one of our record perform-
ances. It is possible that some lame beggar-
woman may rival it, but we are fairly confident
that it will not easily be beaten.

The innkeepers stood at their doors and sur-
veyed us as we passed, more in pity than in contempt ; and we moved on through the town, trying
to judge by the outward appearance whether the
"Lion," the "Hand," the "Goat," or the "Angel"
were nearest what we wished. In this investiga-

tion we were much aided by the peculiar con-
struction of the town. Every house stood alone,
and had a street on every one of its four sides, a
plan which takes a little room, but is handy in the
long-run. We could see no back-yards, no gardens, as we rode round each grey block : the latter,
we afterwards discovered, are kept outside the
town ; the former, and their ashpits, we can only
suppose to occupy some dark and dreadful recess
in the heart of the houses themselves.

The landlord of the "Angel" looked at us and
the Tommies with a horsey and indulgent smile,
as we passed him for the second time. His wife
was remarkably like one of Miss O'Flannigan's
aunts. Moved by these considerations, we yielded
ourselves to the ostler and staggered into shelter.

CHAPTER V.

" I THRAVELLED a dale when I had th' influenzy."

That was how a County Waterford gardener described the delirious wanderings of fever. It also describes our state when the momentary joy of receiving our luggage from the station had passed, when the long process of dressing was over, and we lay, speechless victims of headache, on our beds. To the feverishness of heat and exhaustion was added the gliding panorama of mountain and wood and glaring sky, items of our ignoble twelve miles; they became abhorrent, and yet the brain toiled to fill in any forgotten feature. Such was the result of the Indian method of dealing with hot weather.

It was dealt with that afternoon in a more

efficient manner. In the first place, a parasol
was bought from the leading draper, a pink silk
one, reduced from three-and-nine to two shillings,
on account of the places where it had faded
yellow. It was certainly a bargain, and an hour
afterwards the barometer began to fall, very
slightly, but sufficiently to show intelligence.
Next morning the heat was still supreme, but
this was in order that we might spend another
two shillings on puggarees, after which the
barometer fell a little more.

The shops of Dolgelly have the great advantage
of a street on all four sides of each house, each
standing "a tower of strength, four square, to
every wind that blew," so that bread, boots,
millinery, vegetables, and patent medicines can
command each a window, great or small; and
the shopkeeper stands, Argus-eyed, in the centre,
and caters for the enigmatic needs of tourists,
much as a missionary might prepare glass beads
for the Central African. Each shopkeeper knows
his customers, to the last farmer's wife; they

are united to him in a bond inferior only to
matrimony, as the interloper, of however long
standing, finds to his cost.

" If you could get it anywhere else you wouldn't
come 'ere for it," said a shopkeeper in our hearing, apostrophising the departing figure of a
casual purchaser. " I'm 'ere twenty-five years,"
he went on, wiping the flies off a perspiring piece
of bacon with his pocket - handkerchief, " and
they 'ave as little likin' for me as the first day I
took down my shutters, because I'm English. Ah,
the Welsh stand together, they do, and they 'ate
the English. They're near, too—terrible near."

It was no more than ten o'clock in the morning, and yet when we emerged from the shop,
a " Rehoboth " was sending a stentorian hymn
forth through the town, and the streets were full
of people hurrying to it. The tune was wild
and stately, and the minor phrases followed
each other unfaltering. We insensibly drew towards the door, and listened while the slow
melody rose and dropped like a path in the

mountains—a path washed with mountain rain
and purified with mountain wind. Within, the
people stood close in the hideous pews, in the
naked galleries; three men in black coats, sta-
tioned in three rostrums high up against the white
wall, led the singing, and evidently found the
weather too hot. We observed that their eyes
were upon us, and that an elder seemed to be
developing a tendency to offer us a Welsh
hymnal, and we retired.

The morning was obviously one to sacrifice to
expeditions, and any tourist worthy of the name
would no doubt have been by noon on the top of
Cader Idris or the Torrent Walk. The landlady
of the " Angel," looking more than ever like Miss
O'Flannigan's aunt, urged us to these and other
courses with veiled reproach, as she would have
reminded the impenitent of evening service, but
the hills in whose lap Dolgelly lies remain unex-
plored by us. Others have been more conscientious ; to them be the glories of accomplishment
and the fell privileges of description. The one

E

and only thing that Miss O'Flannigan desired to
see was a Welsh woman in a Welsh hat; but this,
the landlady was forced to admit, was the one
and only thing not procurable in Dolgelly. There
was the sextoness of the church, an octogenarian,
who had preserved her mother's hat—perhaps she
would do. In half an hour Miss O'Flannigan was
driving the octogenarian before her, carrying a
band-box as old and yellow as herself; and the
rest of the morning was spent in the seclusion of
the hotel garden, where, seated on an upturned
bucket, the octogenarian balanced the heirloom
upon her spotted cap, while Miss O'Flannigan
produced studies of her that were more forcible
than polite.

I, no less enjoyably to myself, sat on a wheel-
barrow in the stable, and laid down the law to
the landlord, the ostler, and the saddler about
"chambering" the stuffing of one of the saddles
so as to fit certain swellings which had appeared
on Tom's back, which might be the result of
warbles, or of an ill-fitting saddle, or of the sudden

The sextoness of Dolgelly.

rise to the dignity of oats, but were certainly
capable of unpleasant developments. Tommy's
hard, yellow hide remained unaltered by saddle,
oats, curry-comb, or any other of its new condi-
tions. Looks were not his strong point, but we
already relied on him—and there was something
attractive in the conscientious way in which he
shied at gate-posts, cows in the field, and other
startling and irregular objects.

It was already far in the afternoon when we rode
out over the bridge at Dolgelly, where a single
trickle of water crept through the central arch.
The sky had mackerel backs in it, the trees stirred
delicately to a newly awakened breeze, and the
barometer was still falling. The puggarees were
packed up, and the pink parasol was furled, but
they were doing their appointed work, and the
change came slowly nearer. In the meantime we
went on and up through wooded glens, past the
ideally placed little fishing hotel of Thynn-y-Groes,
in clear, genial sunshine, without a horse-fly; and
gradually the vague headache, *réchauffé* from the

well-cooked one of yesterday, melted away in that
perfect ride.   The road was lonely, more lonely
than a by-road in West Galway, and, as in Galway,
low hazels grew thickly behind the stone walls;
the wide lowlands down on our left lay sweet and
placid, and silent except for the corncrake; the
mountains ran like a blue wall along the west,
a wall hacked and gashed as if by a siege, but
still indomitable.   Cader Idris blocked the end
of the valley, overlooking all things; but of what
avail are names, to what purpose the narrow English
language?   They will not give one breath of the
transcendent air, or the greenness of the leaves that
the goats were tearing from the hazel twigs, or
one moment out of the heavenly silence.

Descending leisurely from the heights and their
crisp, ragged woods, we discovered a line of railway,
and farther on a desolate hillside village, called by
its inhabitants "Trowsefunneth."   How they spell
it is a different affair; probably they do not try.
We had tea there.   The proprietor of the inn wished
us to have a leg of mutton—"quite tender, yess

indeed! been in the 'ouse a week "—but we thought
this would be high tea with a vengeance, and
accepted the inevitable in its usual form of " 'am-
an'-ecks." We can no longer refrain from mentioning that there are two things in Wales, yea, three,
which the traveller would do well to avoid, and
yet can hardly hope to escape from—butter, bacon,
coffee,—all are bad, even odious ; the bacon salt,
tough, stringy ; the butter yellow, coarse, and, if
possible, more salt than the bacon; the coffee a
shade worse than the ordinary drug supplied by
the British hotel-keeper—and what has already
been referred to as the narrow English language
holds no epithet that will fitly stigmatise British
hotel coffee.

It was past seven o'clock when the reckoning
was paid, and we could have wished we were going
to stay on in the little parlour with the German
coloured prints, and the clatter of Welsh outside
in the kitchen, but it could not be. Already
the ascent of Snowdon was coming into the near
future, a matter of the day after to-morrow, and

the mackerel backs were in the sky. The reluc-
tant Tommies were drawn from their lair, where
the village sat in conclave on them and the hold-
alls, and we pushed onwards by what the proprietor described as "Mr Oakley's privvat road
through the glen." Those who know the Dargle,
in the county of Wicklow, know what a glen can
be at its best, and it is hard to admit that it has
a rival; but in the evening light, with the deep
places of that bosky cleft showing a writhing twist
of white water a hundred feet below, Mr Oakley's
glen was very hard to beat. It was as nearly dark
as the summer night knew how to be when the
loafers of Mahntooroch—this is again the phonetic
gasp of despair—took their pipes from their mouths
to point out to us the way to the Grapes Hotel.
We could make out that it was a sophisticated
village, hemmed in between a wooded hill and a
river, and lying silent in the velvet gloom, except
for the noise of running water and the irregular
patter of the Tommies' hoofs.

A scarlet face loomed in the entry of the hotel
as we slid stiffly from our saddles, and afterwards,
in the sitting-room, we found it burning like a red
lamp at the central table. We fell into converse
with its owner, while from a dark corner of the
room a sickly jingle apprised us that some one was
playing "The Man that broke the Bank at Monte
Carlo."

"My friend's playin' there," explained the tourist with the roast face; "'e's rather a shoy cha-ap."

He further informed us that he came from Man-
chester and 'ad just bin up Snowdon. Perhaps he
did not mean to be discouraging: his intentions
were obviously of the best, and possibly his com-
plexion had something to say to the lurid light in
which he regarded our project of riding the Tommies up Snowdon. Nevertheless, as we heard how,
not three years before, a pony had slipped and
fallen down a precipice, how he himself had felt
"that sick and giddy" at one place that on the
downward path two guides had enveloped his head

in a sack and carried him past the dreaded spot,
and of how insuperably beset with clouds the topmost peak had been, our hearts fell into our boots,
and the tune of "The Man that broke the Bank at
Monte Carlo" has, ever since that night, held a
horror for us that is not entirely its own.

The tourist at the Grapes Inn, Maentywrog.

Between Trawsfynydd and Maentywrog.

CHAPTER VI.

IT was the longest day of the year,—so said the penny almanac in the Mahntooroch Hotel. So, with richer certainty, did we ourselves asseverate before nightfall. Before 9 A.M. the Tommies and their lop-sided burdens had been launched on their twelve miles' journey to Beddgelert ; and we, something depressed in spirit by the farewell warnings of our friend the roasted tourist, were hardening our hearts to the ascent of Snowdon.

We rode up through the Plas Oakley Woods,

along the ramparts of the glens, and reaching higher levels, came on a vision of a mountain lake dreaming in the early sun. Three or four coots beat a silver path across it with their black wings, in alarm that testified to the rarity of the June tourist, and the pine-woods round it still held the purple shadows of morning. Out on the bare hills beyond it the heather was in bloom, and the wind's freshness was softened by the scent of it. The Tommies crawled along with well-considered sluggishness. They had by this time a complete mastery of our characters. In the mornings they found that we were too light-hearted to resent their laziness, and in the evenings too humane. This, and the fact that Miss O'Flannigan made from Tom's back a sketch of nothing in particular, may account for our having taken five hours over the twelve miles. However, it may be conceded that they were hilly miles, and were withal as circuitous in their approach of a given point as an Irishman in getting to the focal point of a bargain. Indeed, one turn of the road looked as if it might have

Miss O'Flannigan made a sketch from Tom's back.

supplied the Irishman himself, when it led us past a dreary cabin whose ambition to be rectangularly frightful yielded to the prior necessity of being crooked in a manner that we thought to be achievable only by the Irish cottage architect. With squalid, squinting eyes it leered aside upon its cabbage-garden and the pigs that rooted therein, and outwards to the sea down a bare valley. We were sensible then, for the first time, of a greyness that was blunting the sunshine, and the cabin with its malign, dirty face seemed responsible for it.

The extremes of landscape met where tumbled heaps of grey rock slanted down from the sky to the flat boggy plain that runs out to Port Madoc. That the road should be protected from these suspended avalanches by a single strand of wire-fencing is a fact that no doubt admits of explanation, but at a cursory view of things its object was not apparent. The loneliness was absolute, whether we looked inland to crags and oak-woods, or sea-ward along the marshes, but by this time we did not expect anything except loneliness. Coventry

F

on a memorable occasion was not more straitly
penned behind its shutters than was Wales as we
rode through it.　The wayside villages seemed
asleep, the farmhouse doors were shut, and the
silence of the roads was comparable only to that
supremest of earth's silences when one is thrown
out of a run, and hounds, riders, and runners have
seemingly passed away into eternity.

Turning inland again among the low oak-woods,
the country was rich and flowery, and always
silent, and we ourselves were hot and speechless
under the hot, grey sky.　A discovery that one of
the girths was rubbing off the skin behind Tom's
foreleg occasioned a delay fraught with gloom,
difficulty, and the tongues of buckles.　Miss
O'Flannigan mounted a rock, and fell to sketching
the unsketchable—a habit with her in moments of
inglorious crisis, her sole contribution to the difficulty being a stout square of chamois leather
which she wore on her chest in memory of a de-
parted cold.　With this interesting relic I padded
the girth, and we proceeded in despondency.　It
was one of the junctures when the Tommies, and

riding-tours generally, became intolerable, and we were on the dangerous verge of admitting as much, when our attention became concentrated on six black objects advancing towards us in single file along the barren perspective of road. They were a walking party, evidently engaged in record-breaking, and as with purple, streaming faces they swung past us, we accepted the object-lesson, and thanked heaven for the Tommies.

Following on this was a mile of solitude and sinuous advance through craggy places; then, suddenly, the Pass of Aberglaslyn, and the tourist by companies—especially the clerical tourist. There were four long black coats, and as many soft black felt hats, on or about Aberglaslyn bridge, each with a remarkable proportion of female adherents, to whom, guide-book in hand, or with the unaided gush of inspiration, they defined the beauties of the Pass. We are naturally modest, but we cannot refrain from mentioning that from the moment we came in sight we usurped the position of the beauties of the Pass. The adherents of the clergy turned with ecstasy from the

contemplation of nature to feast their eyes upon
us, our sun-burned straw hats, our equally sun-
burned noses, and our bulging wallets.

We are disposed to deal leniently with an un-
successful rival, and inured though Aberglaslyn
must now be to picturesque description, we will
spare it further adjectives.   There was a poor
woman once in the county of Cork who was
shown a dazzling array of wedding - presents.
Speech first failed her, and then she said : " Mother
of God ! it's like a circus."   Thus, and with such
a humble reverence, do we say of Aberglaslyn
Pass, that it is like a circus.

There is something at once gallant and touching
about the way in which the English tourist places
his hand in that of convention, and is led by her,
uncomplaining, through very arid places.   This
elderly generalisation does not, by so much as a
backward glance, include Aberglaslyn, with its
cliffs and fir-trees, and mountain-sides flushed with
blossoming heather ; it is for the moment concentrated upon the grave of Gelert, its railings and

little stone pillars, erected possibly by the Town
Commissioners to supply a want long felt by

tourists of an object for a short walk. The selec-
tors of the site have been carried away by a

sense of fitness probably adhering since the days when they buried their pet rabbits in the back-garden, and, with guileless convention, they have erected the tomb of Gelert under a tree, a healthy one in the prime of life, standing discreetly and yet conveniently in a roadside field. The senti-ment of the back-garden has been added at a touch by the railing, and the result suffices to the tourist. Forth to it, in duteous pilgrimage, go the brides and bridegrooms, seeking in the long vague fore-noons of holiday for some occupation that shall savour of the compulsory, and at all events make them glad to get home again for luncheon. The mile of road between Gelert's grave and his village was punctuated with the newly married ; and, even at the risk of supporting another conventionality, it must be recorded that the distance that separated each bride from her groom was noticeable, and seemed to indicate a desire to economise con-versation.

Do the brides and bridegrooms support the venerable fraud who sits outside the Goat Hotel

in full Welsh costume, selling rag-doll replicas of
herself? It would seem so, for she apparently
prospers, and we cannot believe that the hotel-
keepers, who form the balance of the population,
can buy many rag dolls.

The sky had grown grey, the air chilly, the
weather was turning nasty, the saddles had perceptibly turned and were extremely nasty. These
things may perhaps extenuate our bad taste in
finding Beddgelert a trifle disappointing. It
seemed to lack a central point; even the guide-
books have to admit that its lions are not on the
spot, although it seductively adds that they are
within an "easy walk." Snowdon was also included among the objects of interest within an
easy walk, but a brief colloquy with the manageress of the Prince Llewellyn Hotel stamped the
statement as a vicious flight of fancy.

"It's a good four miles," said that intelligent
woman, regarding us compassionately; "but there
is ladies that think nothing of that."

We hastened to assure her that we were not of

such, and a few moments of confidential discussion
at the bar sufficed for a programme superior to
any that the guide-books had to suggest. It is
in such affairs as these that the landlady and the
coffee-room-maid show qualities not to be found
in the landlord, or even the ostler. They can rise
above convention ; they have an instinctive percep-
tion of what the tourist, in his bewildered heart,
prefers, but fears to acknowledge ; and they are
capable of giving advice with a sound disregard
for the logic of precedent. Therefore it befell
that our bones are not now bleaching on the
"Beddgelert ascent" of Snowdon, and that, after
a large cold lunch, which included a delicious
but embarrassingly stony cherry - pie, we found
ourselves riding slowly towards the village of
Rhyddu.

This was the scheme of the manageress. We
were to ride on to Rhyddu, leave the ponies at
the Quellyn Arms, get a guide, and having ascended
Snowdon by the shortest route, sleep on top, see
the sun rise, and be back at Rhyddu for break-

fast. It was almost alarming in its simplicity, and
in the way in which it degraded the ascent of the
highest mountain in England and Wales into a mere
episode of the late afternoon. But, with a baro-
metrical future so uncertain that, as Miss O'Flannigan's cook is in the habit of saying, "you couldn't
tell a day from an hour," its merit was too obvious
to be disregarded.

Low as we had sunk in the social scale, we yet
retained just enough self-respect to preserve us
from asking the rare passer-by which of the misty
bulks that confronted us was Snowdon; but none
the less, we should have liked to know. Snowdon had been to our minds a lonely autocrat, unmistakable as Vesuvius or Fuji-yama; but here
were four or five round-shouldered monsters, all of
about the same height, and none quite as monstrous as we had expected. We settled on several,
and tried successively to make the best of them,
and to experience the sensations of awe which the
guide-book assured us were inevitable under the
circumstances; but the telegraph wire that had

been given as our clue still led us onwards, and
the village of Rhyddu seemed, like all our des-
tinations, to have pitched its moving tent a mile
beyond our estimate.

At length a line of unlovely grey houses stood
by the roadside on a broad green ridge, the telegraph wire sent a feeler down into one of these,
and a modest signboard presently introduced to
us the Quellyn Arms. It was a very small hotel
indeed, but it contained a smell of fried bacon
that would have filled St Paul's, and an ignorance
of the English language that was almost equally
stupendous. We were at this moment on a flank
of Snowdon, as we stretched our stiff legs along
the horse-hair chairs; the terminus of the Snowdon Railway was above us, within a stone's-
throw, and a toy train was curling incredibly
round corners and down into a green valley that
was dovetailed in among the great roots of the
mountain. Outside the parlour window a thick-
set figure with a long stick waited immovably
—as immovably as Snowdon, or as the misty

The Snowdon guide outside the parlour window.

cloud in which its horns were plunged. As we momently grew stiffer, the probability that the sun would rise next morning seemed slighter than usual, and we tried to persuade the thick-set man to regard the position from our point of view. But a Snowdon guide has an optimism about sunrises, and a conviction in the matter of a bird in the hand being worth two in the bush.

This, we were assured, was the longest day in the year. It would be light all night. There was a very good hotel on the top to which he, Griffith Roberts, had guided forty people the night before, all of whom had seen Ireland, Scotland, and the Isle of Man at sunrise.

Miss Jones, the landlady's daughter, interpreted these things to us, and we recognised compassion in her eye as she did so. Our craven hearts sank low; but we realised that, as Mark Twain has sufficingly expressed, we must "crowd through or bust."

CHAPTER VII.

THE ascent of Snowdon began as seductively, as gently, as the first step towards a great crime. A grassy cart - track curved idly through pastures that had just a perceptible heavenward tendency, enough to stimulate the traveller and flatter his vigour and prowess. The air was bland and sweet, and the clouds that had been solemnly seated on the mountain began to move away in vagrant wisps and shreds, baring the ponderous side and shoulder and the white track that climbed them at what we considered an absurdly easy gradient.

Griffith Roberts had allotted us but brief time for rest or refreshment at the Quellyn Arms. As the clock struck seven he had tapped fatefully at

the parlour window, and we had followed him as
unresistingly as the rats followed the Pied Piper.
There are, however, rare occasions when it is
agreeable to be coerced into doing what is right.
As, at a steady three and a half miles an hour,
we strode after Griffith Roberts, we began to be
conscious of restored enthusiasm and intelligence,
and, impartially, it seemed to us that we should
be delightful charges for him—so affable, so active,
so anxious for information. Griffith Roberts's back
had, however, not quite so social an aspect as
might have been expected, and he maintained his
lead of five yards with uncommunicative firmness.
Miss O'Flannigan and I called on each other for
a spurt, and for two or three minutes walked at
the rate of four miles an hour without any appreciable result. It became clear that Griffith Roberts moved, planet-like, in a certain fixed relation
to his satellites, and that his lead of five yards was
an institution not easily to be set aside. All that
we had effected was the raising of the pace from
three and a half miles to four, and the discovery

that the grasshopper, or its equivalent, the hand-satchel, had become a burden. Griffith Roberts might scorn us as companions, but he should not ignore his duties as a hireling. We hailed him, and having bestowed the satchel upon him, Miss O'Flannigan made a determined plunge into conversation.

"I suppose you have often been up Snowdon?" she began, in the strong, loud voice which is believed to force comprehension on the foreigner.

She had to say it thrice, and Griffith Roberts finally replied, "Oh yess, one time."

This was a confession of startling frankness ; and Miss O'Flannigan and I, recalling in a lightning-flash the Mahntooroch tourist's tales of incompetent guides, and of a clergyman whose bones had been picked clean by Snowdon wild cats, regretted that our five-shilling fee had been squandered upon an amateur.

"And yesterday," continued Griffith Roberts, after a pause, during which I suppose he was mustering his English vocabulary, "it wass two times also I wass on taap."

"He means he's been up once already to-day!" expounded Miss O'Flannigan in a whisper, whose breathlessness was doubtless caused by her surprise. Griffith Roberts must himself be kin to the wild cats if he could go up Snowdon twice in the day at a speed of four miles an hour, and I began to admit to myself that a guide of this description might perhaps be thrown away upon us. Something infirm, with asthma, we would gladly have put up with; we should even have overlooked a club-foot. At about this period the cart-track began to show symptoms of having had enough, and of wanting to turn back. Fadingly it led us to a wall and a wicket-gate, such as occurs in 'The Pilgrim's Progress,' and it and its grassy ruts were seen no more.

That which replaced it was a simple adaptation of the bed of a stream to the uses of a road. Dry it certainly was, but whether the bed of a stream be wet or dry, it is not easy to walk upon. We

followed the example of Griffith Roberts, whose
regard for his boots seemed his one human weak-
ness, and climbed after him through the heather
tussocks along the bank. Single file and silence
prevailed severely, and my heart began to beat
in unusual places, such as my throat and ears.
What Miss O'Flannigan's heart did I could not
tell, but each time that I caught from behind a
glimpse of her cheek, it seemed to glow in more
royal contrast to the dull background of the
mountain - side. Another wall and wicket - gate
were arrived at; our guide looked round at us
with an eye of cynical expectancy, and hesitated.
It was an intimation that we might rest,—a com-
passionless concession to the inadequacy whose
extent he knew by experience, and not by sympathy. But sympathy was not what we craved
for. I sat down on a rock, and Miss O'Flannigan
extended herself at full length on some contiguous
boulders, and the 'Arabian Nights' could not have
provided us with any more satiating form of enjoyment.

Half-way Miss O'Flannigan extended herself at full length on some contiguous boulders.

We were already far above Rhyddu; its slate
roofs were but grey specks on the green slant of
the valley, the mountains behind it had dwindled
to hills, and other green valleys with dark lakes
in their bosoms had appeared, crowding round
the feet of Snowdon. It was a fine view, and
there was plenty of it, and it had for the first
minute or two the peculiarity of moving in earth-
quake leaps that kept time to the thumping pulses
of my head. It quieted down gradually, and Miss
O'Flannigan, faint yet pursuing, addressed herself
again to conversation and Griffith Roberts.

"Are there many eagles on Snowdon?" she
began in a slow shout.

Griffith Roberts was examining the scenery with
a still eye of cold recognition, and said, "Oh yess,
indeed," which by this time we understood to be the
Welsh manner of expressing want of comprehension.

"Eagles! Big birds, you know!" screamed
Miss O'Flannigan.

The guide shook his head, and again said, "Oh
yess."

Miss O'Flannigan got up from her boulders.

"Big birds!" she repeated, "with beaks like this"—she put her forefinger to her forehead, and described thence a brilliant outward curve —"with big wings"—she flapped her arms violently—"big birds who steal lambs!"

"Ah," said Griffith Roberts, "ze *fahxes!* Oh yess, many fahxes."

Miss O'Flannigan sat down again, and I laughed a great deal.

Having identified the winged and beaked Snowdon foxes, Griffith Roberts displayed no further intelligence, nor, indeed, did Miss O'Flannigan; and after another minute's grace we were crawling again up the dark, heathery slope that at each step grew steadily steeper. I was full of determination, but I did not enjoy myself, and I began to have grave doubts on the subject of getting the "second wind" fabled by the athletic. Lightly had we persuaded ourselves that days spent during previous winters in following hounds on foot over the mountain-sides of West Cork would have been

ample preparation for Mont Blanc. The West
Cork fox is a gentleman, and has a consideration
for his followers that was undreamed of by Griffith
Roberts. Heather tussock, slippery grass, loose
stones, shelving rock, came in steep succession
as unending as the rungs of Jacob's ladder, all
of them achievements in their turn, each one
rather more so than the last. In fact, Jacob's
ladder, or any other frankly precipitous thing,
where one could have been helped by one's hands,
would have been preferable to the short cut by
means of which Griffith Roberts abbreviated, and
at the same time imparted, the bitterness of death
to the ascent.

The air became perceptibly sharp as we went
up, and scraps of cloud floated near us across the
delusive stretches of desolation. Everything was
harmoniously huge: the Eiffel Tower, perched on
one of the crags, might have restored to the eye
some sense of the human scale of measurement;
but to think of feet—even of the guide's, of which
it might truly be said that "a deal of his leg had

been turned up when they were made"—was an
idle effort of memory. It was half an hour before
our guide paused again; the short cut, and we
with it, had climbed a moraine of boulders, and
rejoined the orthodox path, and a rest came as an
unlooked-for mercy.

"Ferry deep," said Griffith Roberts, leaving the
path and moving cautiously towards a low grassy
rampart, behind which the mist steamed billow-
ing up.

We knelt with our elbows on the rampart, and
saw chaos heaped in grey vapour below—chaos
stirred as if with a ladle, and weltering slow and
mysterious in the perfect quiet of the air. As we
watched, some unseen force from below tore an
upward opening through the mist, and our nerves
dived tingling down it to where, at the bottom of
all things, a little leaden lake lay dead and sombre.
The cliff on which we were kneeling ran with
a tremendous horse-shoe curve right up to the
highest peak of Snowdon, a point darkly visible
in the greyness, and depressingly remote. Could

The ascent of Snowdon.

that infinitesimal dot be the hotel that had held forty people the night before?

It was Miss O'Flannigan who made the contemptible suggestion that we should return to Rhyddu and get particulars of the sunrise and the view from the landlady's daughter. I repelled the suggestion with appropriate spirit ; but half an hour later, when, with acute neuralgia in the muscles above my knees, I was reduced to lifting each leg in succession with my hands, I hardly dared to think of the horse-hair sofa in the parlour of the Quellyn Arms. As we dragged ourselves up at the pace relentlessly demanded by Griffith Roberts, all sense of connection with the world below went from us. It was weeks since we had supped at Rhyddu, years since the tourist shouted his final warnings after us at Mahntooroch. We were in another planet, toiling up through some dim, endless purgatory to ever higher levels in the manner so trimly arranged by the newer Spiritualism — only that instead of the corresponding moral elevation, the one emotion in which we were conscious of any progress was detestation of Griffith Roberts. A sodden twilight, not born of sunset or moonrise, came down about us, and the tormented vapours writhed up to meet it from the voids on either hand as we went delicately along the ridge that leads, like a horse's crest, from shoulder to summit of the mountain. The ridge grew more and more slender, and we picked our aching steps more and more carefully. One of the Tommies' saddles would have been almost wide enough to have spanned it comfortably at one place—the happy Tommies, now doubtless sleeping like infants in their little beds at Rhyddu; and Miss O'Flannigan has since admitted her almost uncontrollable desire to traverse it after the manner of a serpent.

It was half-past nine o'clock when Griffith Roberts led his now speechless prey up to the tiny plateau whereon were a large cairn of stones, two men, and two squalid wooden shanties.

"Ze taap," observed Griffith Roberts, coldly.

CHAPTER VIII.

A SOLITARY candle struggled with the obscurity
as we stumbled through a narrow door into the
shanty indicated to us. It illuminated principally
the features of a young gentleman in a check
ulster and a Tam o' Shanter cap, who sat behind
it with a note-book and pencil and an indefinite
air of being connected with the Press, and his
eye-glasses flashed upon us with almost awful
inquiry as the light caught them beneath the
dashing tilt of his cap. The next most immedi-
ate impression was of the cabin of a fifth-rate
coasting steamer : dingy wooden walls, a bare
seat running round them, two tables, three
cramped doorways, and a pigmy stove. That
was the sum-total of the surroundings ; but the

fact that there was a fire in the stove crowded
out all deficiencies for the first ten minutes.

The cold was clinging, inescapable, unbelieve-
able, at least for people who had come sweltering
up in light attire from a world where it was midsummer and behaved as such. The opening of
the stove was about as large as the lens of a
Kodak, and might have heated us through if
moved up and down our persons, as a painter
burns old paint off with a brazier. Failing this,
we had to reverse the process, and rotate endlessly
before that single, sullen glow, while from the
corner the twin malignity of the double eye-
glasses blazed upon us.

"I thought I was goin' to be all alone up here
to-night," said a voice from behind the eye-glasses
—a voice of that class which, like Scott's poetry,
"scorns to be obscure," and proclaims its natal
Brixton in clarion tones. "I've bin kicking my
'eels up 'ere since five o'clock, and I cawn't say
it's bin lively!" The speaker permitted to himself a dramatic yawn, followed by a giggle of

"The speaker permitted to himself a dramatic yawn."

incipient boon-companionship, but the conversation was not given time to expand with the luxuriance of which it was doubtless capable. The door of the cabin was opened, and Griffith Roberts stood without, waiting for his lawful five shillings, and, subsequently, the price of a drink (which, in deference to our possible scruples, was entitled " ginger-beer "). We bade him good-bye without a pang. He is a good man, and would be invaluable as hare for a paper-chase ; but if we ever ascend Snowdon again—which Heaven forfend—it will not be under his guidance.

We stood at the door and watched him go down and down through the lifeless twilight, till the cold bit through and through our summer coats and linen shirts, and a precept of early youth rose menacingly in our minds :—

> " Whatever brawls disturb the street,
> Wear flannel next your skin."

What if we both developed influenza on the top of Snowdon ! Some preservative was instantly

H

necessary: we hurriedly appealed to the proprietor of the cabin for hot water, and were
supplied with a boiling jugful on the spot.
The Summit Hotel does not go in for style,
but it understands the mystery of boiling water,
which is a thing too deep for many of its
betters.

I have often had cause to curse the day on
which it was revealed to Miss O'Flannigan, by
a palmist, that she was subject to medical inspi-
rations; but even the power of speech was denied
to me for some minutes after I had tasted the
mixture of Bovril, whisky, and hot water, com-
pounded by my companion under the influence
of her latest inspiration. Our fellow-tourist, after
a period of aghast observation, attacked his note-
book with an ardour that convinces us that the
recipe will be made glorious by his pen in the
columns of the 'Brixton Chanticleer.' Then he
drew forth a pipe and tobacco-pouch, and looked
first at the mists which were pressing against
the little port-hole of a window behind his head,

and then at us. We accepted the hint, and retired to the cabin allotted to us.

It was about seven feet square, and contained
a bedstead that covered all the room save a strip
of two feet, on which stood a doll's chest of
drawers with a small jug and basin on it. In
the face of the fact that there was but one other
bedroom, it was idle to speculate as to how the
forty visitors of the night before had disposed
themselves; but a very cursory investigation of
the sheets forced us to the conclusion that many
of them had gone to bed in their boots. Possibly
they were right. Top-boots and an entire suit
of oil-skins would alone have brought those sheets
within the sphere of practical politics. We wrapped
ourselves in the blankets, and lay down, fully clad,
to wait for the dawn.

Never before that night had I known how much
more miserable one may be made by sleep than
by the want of it. The thin doses forced on us
by fatigue had the property of magnifying-glasses,
and turned a vague insufficiency of pillow into a

broken neck, the cold and stiffness into centuries
of Arctic hardship. A monotonous wind sighed
round the shanty, and the small uncurtained window held a changeless square of ghostly light, that,
in the intervals of the fevered dreams of this midsummer's night, became a giant luminous match-
box hanging on the wall beside us. Once or twice
Miss O'Flannigan broached in gloomy monologue
reflections proper to the occasion, their *leit motif*
being that we, the newspaper-man, and the two
shanty proprietors, were the five highest people
in England. I cannot remember that I contrib-
uted to the conversation anything more appropriate than the remark of a slighted Dublin
aristocrat, in vindication of her rights of pre-
cedence, "and me the rankest lady in the room,"
—which, indeed, had only a remote and dream-
like connection with the subject.

The luminous paint in the window-frame was
just perceptibly brighter when the door of the
opposite shanty opened, and we heard a heavy
step outside. By this time we had become re-

conciled to the blankets, and we held our breaths
with the dread that there might be a sunrise,
and that we should have to go out into the
piercing air to look at it. There was a batter-
ing upon the Brixtonian door, and then a voice:
"It's a quarter past three, sir, and it's a *very*
thick morning," and then our heroic fellow-
traveller: "Never mind, I'm comin' out."

We lay, silent as stones, listening intently.
The footstep paused at our door, but relenting,
passed on without knocking. Presently we heard
the newspaper-man go forth like the dove from
the ark, and, after a similarly brief absence, return,
and settle himself down in the saloon, where, faithful to the interests of the 'Brixton Chanticleer,' he
no doubt occupied himself in recording his impressions of the mist. For the sake of our self-
respect we rose and looked out of the window—
a shuddering glance which scarcely revealed to
us the foggy outlines of the other shanty and
the cairn of stones.

Beyond these, a thick curtain of mist without a

fold in it. In the bitter cold and the hideous day-light we shawled ourselves again in our blankets and slept miserably till seven o'clock, when, after such gruesome toilet as circumstances and a small jug of ice-cold water permitted, we emerged from our cabin, objects that our nearest relations would have been justified in cutting. The gentleman from Brixton had gone, and the sun had arrived too late to arrange a sunrise, but still anxious to oblige. There was also a kettle of boiling water, a loaf of bread, and a clear fire in the stove. All these things disposed us to realise with a new benevolence what an achievement of labour and perseverance was embodied in the Summit Hotel. The ponies on whose backs each plank and each lump of coal has been carried up are alone able to estimate that achievement perfectly, but they are not likely to expatiate on it, and the fleshless mountain-track repudiates the hoof - prints that could tell of scramble and struggle.

Outside the shanty, when we stepped into the open air, we found most of Wales, clad in the chilly, opaline tints of morning, waiting in complacent silence for the inevitable burst of admiration. On three sides of it was a hazy shimmer, a misty sparkle, betraying the environing sea, from the river Dee to the Bay of Cardigan, and close about us were the grey spines and huge slants of the Snowdon range. George Herbert, with a fine discrimination, has said—

" Praise the sea, but stay on shore."

And in respectful adaption of this counsel, we would say to those who ascend heights for the sake of the view, that a mountain, in shape, in colour, in sentiment, in every possible aspect, is more praiseworthy from its base than from its summit. Moreover, as to the view itself, it seems to us that a beautiful view is not a mere matter of miles seen from a great height. The world was obviously made to be regarded *en profile*, and not to be stared at, flat-faced, from above; and the view from the top of Snowdon impresses the imagination rather than the sense of beauty. To

look across the tiny hedgerow and homestead
anatomy of the nearer counties, away to England
in the distant haze, was to taste suddenly the
core of many trite sayings about human effort
and insignificance, and in spite of triteness the
great expanse, sown with silent life, was wonder-
ful beyond the symmetry of mountain-peaks.

Many things were revealed to us on the way
down that had been withheld by the mist and
twilight of the ascent.   Ravines into whose purple
shadows the sun had not yet looked—green valleys,
with little lakes lurking in them—white paths
straggling away to every point of the compass—
and pre-eminent and ubiquitous, the soda-water
bottle, the sandwich-paper, and the orange-peel.
It was still October when we started, but now as
we scrambled, slid, and ran with brief, uninten-
tional abandonment down the path, we were
travelling back along the gamut of the months.
By the time we had arrived at the first halting-
place of the night before, our own temperatures
had touched a point that made us independent

of climate; but though we were hardly in a con-
dition to appreciate the balm of mid-June that
was coming up from the pastures, we could not
wish it to be chilled.

Striding up the lower fields, with an ardour
that we recognised compassionately as having
once been ours, were two tourists, a middle-
aged gentleman and his daughter. They paused
as they met us, to unburden themselves of a
kindly platitude or two about the weather; and
it is still on Miss O'Flannigan's conscience that
she gave these harmless wayfarers careful particulars as to Griffith Roberts's short cut, and received their gratitude without compunction.

Shortly after this incident it was that we met
the postmaster of Rhyddu communing alone with
nature—a very noble-looking person, in a costume
modelled upon that of the most sumptuous tourist.
Considering how far we were from the ideal female
of the species, he treated us with unexpected affa-
bility, even giving himself the trouble of accom-
panying us back to the village, favouring us

meanwhile with his political opinions, his low opinion of the Irish race —legitimately founded on a large experience of intoxicated hay‑makers— and other details. He afterwards sold us letter‑cards at a fancy price suggested by ourselves: the problem of the price

"A costume modelled on that of the most sumptuous tourist."

of seven, if nine cost tenpence halfpenny, or some similar sum, being beyond the grasp of the human intellect.

It was 10.30 when we reached the Quellyn Arms, and while the sympathetic Miss Jones pre-

pared cans of hot water and breakfast, we visited
the orphaned Tommies. The Quellyn Arms does
not profess to stable horses, therefore it cannot be
regarded as an unkindness if we mention that the
Tommies were housed in what seemed to be a
lumber-room. Broken things that might have
been beds, washing-mangles, or turnip-cutters,
choked the entrance. One saddle was perched
on a bedpost, like a bonnet on a stand in a shop-
window, the other lay on the ground, and behind
the heap glowered the indignant faces of the
Tommies. Both had pulled their heads out of
their halters, and, in default of other food, were
tearing the stuffing out of an ancient palliasse.
In the boxes that served as mangers were a few
nettles and stalks of mint, sole remnants of some
strange repast which must have borne about the
same relation to hay that curry does to boiled
mutton. The hotel cook strolled into the stable
while we were there; it seemed she had been
hay-making during a pause in the duties of the
cuisine—a fact that recurred to us when subse-

quently the flavour of the hay-fields was perceptible in that of the tea.

The cook at Rhyddu.

She kindly permitted us to fill the mangers of
the Tommies from her private hoard of poultry

corn, and it was on this occasion that we realised
their relation to us was that of rather alarmed
nephews towards severe but conscientious aunts.
There was good feeling on both sides, there was
even a little affection, but the auntly element was
ineradicable.

CHAPTER IX.

THE people of Rhyddu were unanimous on one
point.   They united with enthusiasm to assure us
that there was a short cut to Llanberis, that the
same was easy, and also that it was advantageous.
At this stage of our investigations, however, a
piano-organ with a monkey absorbed the attention
which, till then, had been lavished upon us and
the Tommies—and we left Rhyddu with nothing
better to guide us than an impression of hands
waving vaguely towards a spur of Snowdon, and
some sense of the vital importance of a certain
lane by a farmhouse.

In the course of two miles we attempted three
lanes, and found they all ended alike at a barking
dog and a closed door ; finally, we addressed our-

selves to a pair of shears, which, moved by unseen
hands at the inner side of a hedge, was clapping
its jaws malevolently among the topmost privet
sprouts. There was a small hotel at the other side
of the road, and neither lane nor farmhouse was in
sight ; but a voice from behind the hedge informed
us in unusually fluent English that the short cut
to Llanberis started precisely from the yard of the
hotel. The yard was deserted, but some sem-
blance of a track wandered from it, and we sur-
rendered ourselves to it. It met with an early
death at the gateway of a large, steep field,
unpleasantly filled with cattle and young horses,
and we were on the point of turning back to insult
the man with the shears, when a cow in our vicinity
lay down to ruminate, and disclosed a fat, yellow-
haired boy who had been standing behind her.
To him the stimulating copper was at once ad-
ministered, and under his guidance we pursued an
imperceptible path through the cattle up to the
hill, with a confidence not shared by the Tommies,
who were, indeed, but moderate mountaineers.

At the next field the boy paused, seeming to
consider that we had had our pennyworth ; further
moneys at intervals impelled him upwards to the
highest limits of the pasture-land ; but there, un-
moved even by the sight of sixpence, he left us,
with the information that when we had gone as
high as we could, we should—if we did not lose
our way—find a gate, and from that gate a good
road would take us to Llanberis.   The instructions
had a pleasing simplicity, and, if applied to a tree
or a pyramid, would have been easily followed.
The Snowdon range, however, offers a large selection of highest points, and of these we naturally
chose the lowest and nearest.   The Tommies crept
like beetles athwart the slant of the hill, and we,
our feelings of humanity somewhat blunted by the
exertions of the morning, sat upon their backs, and
saw momently a little more of their persons in front
of us, as the saddles receded towards their tails.

The hill was above us in heather on our left,
below us in steep pasture on the right, and the
Tommies were digging their hoofs into a slanting

ledge between the two. We ascended slowly, clinging to the ponies' manes, I in advance of Miss O'Flannigan, who was in one of her most conversational moods, and demanded my frequent appreciation of the landscape with an enthusiasm that seemed to me ill-timed. Each time I so much as turned my head, the saddle and the hold-all turned sympathetically with me, and I was in the act of ignoring an appeal to my æsthetic feelings when Miss O'Flannigan's voice ceased abruptly. This was so unusual an occurrence that I took a fresh handful of the mane and looked round. Miss O'Flannigan was standing on her head on the off-side of her pony, on whose back nothing was now visible except the girths, while beneath his body hung the hold-all. What it was that formed the link between him and Miss O'Flannigan was not apparent, but as he was eating grass with unshaken calm it was not a matter of vital importance.

Before I had dismounted and reached the scene of the disaster Miss O'Flannigan was free: she had, in fact, rolled over the edge of the ledge into

I

a clump of heather, and was emerging from it, hatless, and in a state of the highest indignation. There is an unconscious, undesired picturesqueness about a person whose hair has come down, and I did not altogether refrain from mentioning this to Miss O'Flannigan, but she had lost her interest in the picturesque. The Tommies, fortunately, viewed the affair from one aspect only—that of a heaven-bestowed interval for food ; and during the arduous processes of re-saddling and of binding the hold-alls, like burnt-offerings, to the horns of the saddles (for we had determined upon walking till we reached the top of the hill), they did not give us a moment's anxiety.

No eyes but those of the aghast, black-faced sheep and the coldly interested carrion-crows witnessed the occurrence, or the subsequent procession upwards, over slippery grass and through the boundless quagmires caused by a stream that seemed newly spilled on the face of the hill, and was still wandering in search of a bed. The hut on the top of Snowdon was visible—an angular atom, retaining even, as a silhouette of the eighth of an inch square, its air of *gamin* self-sufficiency and adequacy for its position of overseer to England and Wales. With the aid of field-glasses, it and its inmates might have come to the conclusion that two aproned and gaitered Deans of the Church of England were leading a pair of heavy - laden sumpter - palfreys over the pass to Llanberis, or might eventually have made the discovery that the most simple manner of adapting a riding-habit to mountain walks is not necessarily the most graceful.

From our private point of view it seemed many times that we had gone as high as was possible before we found the gate that was to compose all difficulties. It linked two long strips of grey wall that had striven towards each other from afar, down mountain flanks and up from boggy valleys, like two lives fated to meet and overcoming circumstance. Their juncture was, as the boy had truly said, on the highest point of the hill ; and leaning breathless on the gate, while the

Tommies tore at the wiry little rushes which grew
all about, we looked down a deep, empty valley

The ascent of the Deans.

to open country with the glint of water and the
smoke of villages. A track of two feet wide
sprang from the farther side of the gate and drew

"*Two or three startled, audacious pony faces peering round a pile of boulders.*"

a steady line along the naked, green face of the
valley, outlining the buxom curves like a string
course with an encouraging downward tendency in
it. Gingerly we trod it, each with an excessively
awkward and all-dubious Tommy in tow—while
the slope below, on the right hand, became a great
deal steeper than was pleasant to look at, and that
above, on the left, so pronounced as to preclude
the possibility of walking on it. Emerging from a
shallow scoop in the face of the hill, and paying
more heed to my steps than to my surroundings, I
felt the steady drag of the elder Thomas upon the
reins become a violent full-stop, and was suddenly
aware of two or three startled, audacious pony
faces peering round a pile of boulders at the turn
of the path. They were gone with a whisk of fore-
locks and a rattle of loosened stones; and having
in some measure reassured the deeply scandalised
Tommies, we proceeded, not without some inward
speculation as to what would happen to them, and
to us, if these sylvan cousins of theirs were to come
avalanching round the corner upon us in an unfor-

tunate burst of family feeling. A few steps took
us round the sharp bend of the hill, and we came
face to face with the foe—a dozen tiny ponies,
standing in dramatic attitudes of expectancy, with
heads high in the air, and wide nostrils spread to
the scent of danger. For an instant their wild
eyes devoured us and their brethren of the cap-
tivity, and then Miss O'Flannigan obeyed her
Keltic instincts, and stooped to pick up a stone.
At that world-comprehended and world-respected
signal they turned all at once, as if blown by a
wind, and floated down the green valley - side,
whose steepness we had scarcely cared to look at,
with heads up, manes and tails streaming, and
shoeless hoofs flicking the turf in bounds that
seemed headlong, yet never went beyond control.
In the bottom of the valley they swung to the
right with the incredible oneness of a flock of birds,
and halting, looked up to us and neighed defiance.
The Tommies hurried on without comment.

Shortly afterwards the rain began,—diffidently,
as if it had forgotten how, but the low bosom of

the grey sky was laid against the hills, and the
undisciplined drops did not long want for re-
inforcement. The salmon - coloured Dolgelly
parasol made but a dismal *début* under these
auspices, and glowed with a more and more sullen
flush as the rain soaked through it and dropped
in dirty pink tears from its spikes. Between the
tears I saw little except the endless downward
progress of the path and unprepossessing glimpses
of landscape blind with rain. We mounted the
Tommies and scrambled by many stony descents
and wet fields to lower levels ; a thin cascade
glanced over the black lip of a ravine and dropped
delicately with slanting leaps down a hundred feet
or more ; wet roofs appeared below us, then a
public road, public-houses, public conveyances,
and an intelligent public interest in us and the
Dolgelly parasol. The conclusion that we were a
circus, or some part of one, was immediately and
loudly announced by the infant population ; and
a vivid representation on a poster of a young lady
hovering in pink tights above the foaming manes

of six white horses, explained that the infant mind had lately been educated in such matters.

That we should have fortuitously selected the Snowdon Valley Hotel from among the many others of the long street was, in this connection, a singular instance of hypnotic suggestion. As we turned towards the coffee-room, the landlady, after a moment obviously spent in comparing us with the poster, made up her mind to give us the benefit of the doubt.

"Perhaps you would rather step to the drawing-room," she said, hesitatingly ; and while she spoke the chorus of "The Man that broke the Bank at Monte Carlo" broke forth from the hilarious conversation in the coffee-room, "we have the—a—the circus ladies and gentlemen in there."

CHAPTER X.

A DULL roar vibrated through my dreams at some
unknown hour of the next morning, and with such
faculties as were not absorbed by the feat of slid-
ing head-first down Snowdon on a telegraph wire,
I set it down as being a manifestation of the
circus ladies and gentlemen. Later on I realised
that the circus ladies and gentlemen did not mani-
fest themselves to any appreciable extent before
luncheon-time; and while we sat at a lonely breakfast in the coffee-room, and inhaled through an
open window the rainy wind that was preferable
to the prisoned aroma suggestive of " a wet night,"
the vibrating roar fell at intervals into our moody
silence. Between the gables of temperance hotels,
and through the cold drifts of rain, the sheer face

of a mountain gleamed black as ink, checkered
with angular scars, carved and sliced into precipitous terraces, ridden of blaspheming steam-engines
that vaunted over its defeat with their white
plumes of vapour.   Occasionally a darkly glittering avalanche of slate-rubbish shot downwards
into the lake below, the mountain groaned as its
dead went hurtling to their burial, and the sullen
protest shook the air.   Llanberis seems indifferent
to the fact that the principal feature in its scenery
is being transferred in slices to the roofs of other
people's houses, and in helter-skelter tons to the
bottom of its lake : perhaps it is helpless, and if so
we offer it sympathy.

As has been insinuated, it was a wet day, and
for some time I feared that my influence over Miss
O'Flannigan was not sufficient to dissuade her
from purchasing a species of pall, made of black
painted canvas, and worn as a cape by "the common quarrymen," as she was coldly told by the
lady behind the counter.   The further information,
however, that its price was seven and elevenpence,

caused her to lay it longingly down and ask for an umbrella—"A very bad umbrella," she explained; " the worst kind you have got——"

Economy is a virtue that the Welsh do not encourage in the alien. The shopwoman did not for some time permit herself to believe that what Miss O'Flannigan desired was primarily cheapness, and secondarily extent, and not silver chains, and ouches, and greyhounds' heads carved in the purest bone. Like many another of her race and calling, she was fated to find us commercial disappointments of the most ignoble kind, and forth, with whatever reluctance, came eventually the lustrous alpaca, the gingham that even in youth looks grey and stout, the massive black handle, the gluey fragrance. A subordinate in goloshes, worn over white stockings, brought them in relays from some remote parts of the house,— some apparently from a period of hibernating in a feather-bed, judging by the fragments of down that adhered both to them and to their bearer. With the largest of the ginghams, at one-and-nine,

with two red comforters, such as are worn by
virtuous woodmen in coloured almanacs, and
with a bag of biscuits (bought at the opposite
counter), we retired into the
rain through a doorway gar-
nished with alarming sac-
rifices in flannelettes and
elastic-sided boots, and
hardened our hearts for
the road.

"We retired into the rain."

Bettwys-y-Coed was
twelve miles away,
or even more, as the
landlady warned
us with what we
hope was disin-
terested zeal for
our welfare ; but
even   twelve
miles in the rain seemed preferable to the ladies'
drawing-room with the photograph-books and
the view into the first floor above the opposite

shop, where the hat - trimming department, un-
occupied as ourselves, sat conversationally in the
windows, "nor deemed the pastime slow."

Draped in horse-sheets to keep the saddles dry,
the Tommies presently stood at the door; and
swaddled, like cabmen, in comforters and capes,
we came forth and mounted. During the process
of sorting the reins, the umbrellas, and the tips for
the two ostlers, we could not but be aware of the
guileless enjoyment of the hat department opposite, and the more critical but equally unaffected
interest of the circus ladies and gentlemen at the
window of a ground-floor sitting-room. As we un-
furled the pink parasol and the tent-like gingham
and went down the street like a pair of fungi on
four legs, the chorus that broke from the ground-
floor window was acutely audible :—

> " Oo're ye goin' to meet, Bill?
> '*Ave* ye bought the street, Bill?
> Lorf?—why, I thought I should 'a *died*——"

Our riding-canes were in the hold-alls, but we
kicked the Tommies to a trot and fled. The

temperance hotels and the villas faded into the mist behind, and we were alone.

In the partial shelter of a soaked sycamore the usual, the inevitable, process of altering the girths was carried out, while the drips flopped suddenly on our noses or the backs of our necks, with an untiring sense of humour, and the tips to the ostlers were repented of with more than usual fervour.

To visit the Pass of Llanberis in such weather was an act as unworthy as calling on a stranger during a spring cleaning. Its mountains were dressing-gowned in ragged cloud, its lake turned to a slab of slate, its vista bleared by the cold, thick rain ; but it had still a murky nobility, and streams, long silent, cast themselves from its parapets, and gauged with white streaks the depth of precipice and jutting crag. Upwards in stream-ing gradients rose the road, along the slanting floor of the valley—if indeed the name of valley is not too tender for that rent in the dark heart of the mountain, with its sides strewn with wreckage

of boulders, and its black walls towering implac-
ably, untouched by summer. Upwards also, in
exaggerated dolour, crept the Tommies, as well
aware as we that the hold-alls, in which were our
riding-canes, were following by coach. The stick
of the gingham was indeed a formidable club, but
being swathed in voluminous folds of material, a
blow from it amounted to no more than a cumbrous
caress, and the application of handle, spikes, or
ferrule proved equally ineffective.

Bare green hills followed on Llanberis Pass.
We were high among them in a strong wind that
sang in our teeth, and brought the hard rain
slanting against us. We looked neither before nor
after, and barely spared a sidelong eye for such
things as appeared on either hand. They were
not many. The lonely inn of Pen-y-Gwrd, where
a glimpse was caught of tourists thronging in a
window to snatch this sovereign incident of a day
that might otherwise have ended in a strait-waist-
coat; a herd of pony-mothers with their foals;
a plover wheeling and whistling in the belief that

K

she was leading astray our search for her nest;
then Capel Curig, a scattered village, lying pleasantly and beautifully on the shoulder of a lake-
filled valley.   Through the windows of a big hotel
we saw luncheon lie even more beautifully, but it
could not be thought of. Six miles of mountain
rain had not been thrown away upon us; our
clothes had admitted it at all possible crevices;
the red comforters were inscribing equally red
stripes upon our necks with their wet, harsh folds;
the gingham looked like a widowed vulture, weep-
ing tears of gluey ink upon all things in its vast
circumference.   Better to accumulate all possible
wetness, and spread ourselves irrevocably to dry
at Bettwys-y-Coed.

The road was suddenly lovely at Capel Curig,
and thereafter to Bettwys.   Trees shaded it, deep
glens beside it hid their rivers and waterfalls
under the locked branches of beech and oak, and
the rain dropped more kindly in the still shelter.
We were on the great Holyhead and London
coach-road, along which previous generations had

driven with what cheer they might, after a day or
so spent in sailing from Kingstown to Holyhead.
Many an Irish member thrilled here with inward
rehearsal of the peroration that should shake
Westminster; many a grudging rebel eye looked
for the first time at the roadside life of a country
whose beauty would put Ireland on her mettle to
excel, whose careful tending showed national pride
in a form which probably had not before presented
itself to the rebel mind. Patriot or undergrad-
uate, genius or duellist, the best that Ireland
had to give swung along this road towards London to the tune of sixteen hoofs; the people
of no account stayed at home in those days,
and when genius travels nowadays, third class in
the North Wall train, it could wish that they still
did so.

The spell of that older time hung unbroken on
the broad road, with the river soliloquising, deep-
throated, in the ravine; the time when wind and
limb did the work in a primitive way, and every
stage saw the perfected relation of man and horse.

A swish, a whirr, the sharp sting of a bell, and two black-caped cyclists were upon us from the opening of a by-road, like two humpbacked monstrosities flying out of the book of Heraldry. The next thing that I saw with any distinctness was the mud squirming through my fingers as I clutched the surface of the road in an endeavour to get my legs clear of the saddle ; and the next, as Tommy and I rose simultaneously to our feet, was Miss O'Flannigan and her Tom retiring to the horizon at the rate of twenty miles an hour. The cyclists were also retiring, in the opposite direction, at about sixty miles an hour. Had Tommy been more practised in the art of pivoting suddenly on his hind-legs while trotting downhill, I should probably have been following in Miss O'Flannigan's wake : as it was, an hysterical " slip up " had been the result, and a final wallowing in the mire. My further impressions of the noble old Holyhead coach-road may be summed up in the statement that its mud is white and is mixed with size to give it adhesive quality.

"I clutched the surface of the road."

By the time that I had emptied some of it from my gloves, and rough-dried the saddle and Tommy with a wisp of grass, Miss O'Flannigan had returned, minus the gingham, and with girlishly floating hair. Our subsequent entry into Bettwys was mercifully cloaked by deluge, but it was difficult to bear with dignity the successive eyes of a walking party, trudging in single file away from it— the same walking party on whom we had bestowed a scornful compassion as we met them in the airless heat near Beddgelert. Even on such a day as this the villas and lodging-houses of Bettwys could look nothing else but flawlessly clean and smart, with their clear grey-stone walls and white-frilled window curtains. Between them and the speeding river (whose bridge and island were, even at a glance, familiar as the mainstay of many water-colour exhibitions) we huddled in downpour to the hotel of our choice ; not the Royal Oak, with its legion of waiters and its private road to the railway station, but to the more sympathetic Glan Aber, where the windows were innocent of the rain-bound tourist lady, and the hall unhaunted of her husband.

In half an hour a great part of the sopping bulk that had paused, dripping, in the hall while the landlady decided to take a trade risk and admit it as guests, had been transferred to the kitchen in armfuls, to the laundress in yet further armfuls, and what remained (in my case) was in bed, drinking hot tea that was yellow with cream. The remnant of Miss O'Flannigan was draped with gloomy grace in plaid-shawls of Dissenting Chapel odour, lent, to the best of our remembrance, by the chambermaid's mother.

"Not by appointment do we meet delight and joy, They heed not our expectancy——" And so also not by appointment do we meet the ideal chambermaid—unless, indeed, we are fortunate enough to be her young man—but we met her that afternoon at the Glan Aber Hotel, and hope some day to do it again.

It was late that evening before the hold-alls arrived from Llanberis, and therefore our toilettes for *table-d'hôte* were, as the fashion articles say, dainty confections, composed of a damp habit-skirt, a mackintosh, shirts hot from the hotel laundry, and the severest of the plaid-shawls. It is scarcely to be wondered at that the sole other occupant of the hotel, a godly young amateur photographer, should have awaited us somewhat nervously as we swept through the long room towards a table laid for three, and should have carved the soup and fish with a trembling hand. With the chicken, however, the photographer had almost ceased to look round for our keeper, and a conversation about Thornton Pickard shutters and time-exposures was beginning to thrive at the hands of Miss O'Flannigan, who affects some acquaintance with these things. The evening finished with all the domesticity imparted by a fire in the drawing-room and a display of negatives, Kodaks, shoulder-straps, and other ingredients of a photographic walking tour. We felt that we were a godsend to this good and lonely youth, and parted from him with every hope that on the morrow he would ask

to be permitted the privilege of photographing the
Tommies and the expedition generally.   It was
therefore crushing to find on the morrow that he
had unexpectedly fled at daybreak, with all his
worldly possessions.   He did not know it, but he
was obeying the decree that, Claudian-like, we
should blight the fortunes of every hotel we stayed
at, and reign in malign monopoly of coffee-room
and *table-d'hôte.*

CHAPTER XI.

HITHERTO farewell had been slightly said, with a few backward looks of good feeling, a few civil wishes for an indefinite return. But at Bettwys, for the first time, and perhaps also because it was—of this vagrant expedition—so near the last, parting gave pain. Turning on the face of a hill we looked back over the valley and across the flitting showers to the peaks of Snowdon and Moel Siabod, a retrospect to be remembered and thirstily to be desired in other summers. Darkly and greenly the woods sank into every cleft, or rose with the piled-up landscape till the cold breast of Snowdon was half hidden behind them. A river, whose name is quite immaterial, plunged uproari-ously down to the five crooked arches of Pont-y-

Pair bridge in Bettwys, then, finding itself suddenly
in good society, pulled itself together and swam
tense and flat round a curve to present itself
decorously to what I think we are safe in assert-
ing to be the river Conway. It was true that
half-pay generals and forlorn honeymoon couples
haunted the bridge and hung round the post-office,
that "well-appointed conveyances" were daily
braying forth with horns the multitudinous entry
of the tourist, also that the glass was falling;
none the less we should thankfully have turned
the Tommies down the hill again and remained
without purpose or limit at Bettwys. Then, indeed, might many periods have been instructively
framed around the names of the Miner's Bridge,
the Swallow Falls, and Dolwyddelan Castle, all
of which the guide-book assured us with chaste
esteem were "well worthy of a visit." All that
now remained was to turn away from the parapet
of the wooded precipice, from whose edge we
were looking back, and pace lingering forth towards Corwen.

" The parapet of the wooded precipice, from whose edge we were looking back."

A stertorous sound began presently to be dis-
tinguishable from the hoarse note of rushing water
in the deep places of the glen : then followed a
tremor of the ground, lastly a traction-engine,
advancing upon us like Behemoth throned on
mill-wheels, opulent of smoke, with a clanging
retinue of trucks. I felt in anticipation the mud
ooze again through the seams of my gloves, as it
had oozed last night, but the gate of a villa was
suddenly and miraculously raised up on our left
hand. Miss O'Flannigan was off, and had opened
one-half with a celerity which suggested long
practice in the hunting-field, and we burst through
into the shadow of tall evergreens, tearing out a
hold-all buckle in an encounter with the gate-post.
We were startlingly confronted inside by an old
lady in a mushroom hat, carrying a spud and
garden-basket, and wearing an expression of complete and unaffected amazement, which, considering all things, and especially the fact that Miss
O'Flannigan and I had fallen into maniac laughter,
was a pardonable lapse of good breeding. Point-

ing to the traction-engine, we endeavoured to
explain ourselves; but the chilly calm with which
the Tommies regarded it, as it lumbered past the
gate, was so painfully at variance with our representations, that it seemed better to retire, waving
hysterical apologies.   The old lady stirred neither
hand nor foot throughout the occurrence, and for
all we know may have been a rustic detail added,
in wax, by a proprietor of a realistic turn.

After this the road was quiet in the balmy
quietness of summer, that is so living a thing
compared with the soulless grip of the air in
winter silences. By the dignified gradients of
the coach-road we mounted slowly through woods
and glens, and then, with no less dignity and
almost equal slowness, downwards into open
country, clear and kindly, with pasture, and level
roads, and a wide eastward horizon melting into blue.   Behind us the Snowdon range stood
mightily on the high pedestal of Carnarvonshire :
it had never showed itself so great as now, viewed
from these Denbigh meadow-lands, while we rode

to the east, with faces turning always back to the
splendid barrier across the west.   It was a lonely
road, with scarcely a mark to ruffle its white dust
except the ribbed footprint of the traction-engine,
that stretched like an illimitable ladder in front
of us.   We met no one save two tramps who eyed
us curiously, as members of the fraternity who
ought to be able to impart useful facts about the
temper of the nearest farmer's wife, or the quality
of the skilly at the Llanberis workhouse ; a little
farther on, on a long reach of road, quite remote,
as it seemed, from human habitation, we met three
tall women, dressed alike in widows' weeds, and
each pressing a pocket-handkerchief with a wide
black border to the point of a pink nose.   Their
eyes turned at us above these emblems of woe
with something of interest, but they did not pause,
and went on, three black blots on the white road
between the glowing hedgerows ; and we mar-
velled if some Welsh Mormon elder had lived
and died, unknown, but obviously lamented, in
these sunny solitudes.

L

Pentre Voelas and Cernioge came in their turn,
with mild episode of farmhouse and wayside inn,
and manifold iterance of Rehoboths and Salems.
Cernioge, as we discovered in the buying of a

" *Three tall women, dressed alike in widows' weeds.*"

post-card, is pronounced Kernoggy. This eccentricity was, so far as we could see, its sole claim
to distinction. From the first the Tommies had
established a rule to demand nourishment at every
inn they passed, and after twelve miles studded

with—for them—disappointments, we yielded to
their importunities, and paused at the glowing
sign of the Saracen's Head, Cerrig-y-Druidion.

In the best parlour sat in perfect silence a
tradesman and his wife, middle-aged, serious,
and too entirely respectable to be aware that
they were bored almost to madness. They were
out on their holiday, therefore they were enjoying
themselves—and therefore the tradesman read a
month-old copy of the 'Cyclist,' and his wife studied
the 'Farmers' Gazette,' and both eyed us with raven-
ous, but decently furtive, interest. For half an hour
we and our safety-skirts were vouchsafed to them,
while the familiar tea, with home-made gooseberry-
jam and salt butter, was vouchsafed to us; and
then the Tommies, having polished their mangers
with their usual precision, were led forth again.

It was not a good ten miles that we rode from
there to Corwen, except in the sense of good,
full, statute measure. Disaster fell upon us like
a net, tangling our endeavours with inexhaustible
mesh. A "dee" of my saddle broke; consequently

I had to carry the hold-all across my lap, like a baby of monstrous size and implacable pig-headedness. Tom the elder developed a new and much enlarged edition of his ancient girth-gall, and in the attempt to cope with this by re-saddling, a cushion of swelling was disclosed along his back. Miss O'Flannigan then said she would lead him the rest of the way, and did so, until the next milestone announced that it was four miles to Corwen, which at once degraded the project from the sublime to the ridiculous. Not all the Humane Society, in one throbbing merciful mass, could be absurd enough to expect any one to walk four miles in a riding-habit, and cloth gaiters, and the dog-days.

The cool of the evening was upon us before we at length sighted Corwen across the pastures, and a pale after-glow, pale as the points of gaslight that were starting up about the railway station, gleamed on the long curve of the river Dee as we crawled across the bridge outside the town. Corwen is a dingy, mean town, in spite of the

wooded cliff at its back, and the river at its foot,
and the river meadows with their tranquil sweet-
ness; but on that Saturday night neither we nor
the Tommies complained of its dinginess. It had
a chemist, who kept sulphate of zinc and iodoform,
and lead lotion, with which to anoint the invalid;
and it had a sedate and venerable hotel, the Owen
Glendwr, in which instantly to go to bed. Having risen thus to the occasion, Corwen may be
assured that it has not lived in vain.

Carriages, with Sunday bonnets in them, began
to pass next morning, while yet we were taking
in the delicate antique absurdity of the pair of
spinets in the drawing-room, the charms of the
brass finger-plates and door-handles, the impres-
siveness of the low-ceiled, spotless kitchen, with
the vast fireplace, and all the strong and sound
old age of a house that has been a notable inn
since the fifteenth century. Finding that the
church was immediately behind the hotel, and,
furthermore, that the service was in Welsh, we
lingered a little in the tour of brew-house and

still-room, until the Venite, clear and harmonious,
came across the graves to the wide kitchen window
that leaned its sill on the churchyard grass.

Presently, when seated in the porch of the
church itself, we heard again the rich accord of
Welsh voices, with all their grave and fearless
certainty, their peasant simplicity, their unblem-
ished nationality. Would that many Irish and
English congregations, shrieking in hideous rivalry
half a bar behind the organ, could comprehend
the reticence of strength, the indwelling instinct
of time, and the sense of harmony, manifested
at a Welsh country service, where the children
lisp in altos, and the farm-hand and the butcher's
boy add their tenor or bass with modest assurance.
The preacher's voice was a fine one, and rung and
swung in that strange metrical wail of Welsh that
we had heard before in the church of Mallwydd,
but it lacked something of the melancholy passion
given to that first voice by the touch of age in
the tone, the inference of sadness and misgiving.
Owen Glendwr had a pew in this very church ;

probably was churchwarden, and sanctified while he indulged his predatory instincts by going round with the plate. There seemed something significant in the fact that his dagger is carved on a stone just outside the church : did he, we wondered, employ it as a discourager of threepenny-bits and a stimulator to half-crowns. At all events, he is now the next thing to a saint in Corwen, and his works any inhabitant can tell with chapter and verse in a manner which it is not our intention to vie with.

Among other chief tenets of Corwen morality is the necessity of seeing Llangollen. We had, indeed, been ourselves something fired by quotations from Wordsworth and other competent judges in the guide-book, and yielding to the serious representations of the landlady on the subject, we ordered a small trap in which we might thither drive ourselves and the drab Tommy. As we sat in the embrasure of the coffee-room window, waiting for the entrapped Tommy, we perceived a vehicle resembling a

mammoth governess-cart at the hotel door, with
an old man, dressed in what we had learned to
regard as the height of Welsh religious fashion,
standing by it. His beard was long and white,
his face was cross, with a crossness that momen-
tarily deepened as he glanced at the hotel. We
studied him with the refined observation of idle-
ness.

"An Arch-Druid, evoluted into an elder of the
straitest of the Rehoboths," remarked Miss O'Flannigan, easily ; "his wives and daughters had better
not keep him waiting much longer, there is the
flame of human sacrifice in his eye, pleasantly
blended with the confidence of their eternal——"

At this juncture, Ellen, the coffee-room-maid,
came into the room.

"If you please, ladies, the driver is waiting, and
wants to know when you will be ready."

So we were his wives and daughters! We went
forth anxiously to accept the situation, too depressed even to wrangle as to which was which.

That no trap was available for Tommy was, in

some abstruse way, known to Ellen and explained
by her at some length, the result of the day being
Sunday, as was also the attendance of the Arch-
Druid. We ventured a suggestion that we should
forego the latter privilege and ourselves drive the
stolid black mare, whose massive beam barely
filled the shafts ; but, with a contempt apparently
too deep for words, the Arch-Druid mounted to
the prow of the governess-cart as to a pulpit, and,
manipulating the mouth of the black mare with
the ceaseless, circular action of a hurdy-gurdy
grinder, started at a round pace for Llangollen.

It was a nine-mile drive, and by the time the
eighth milestone had been passed, we began to
look for some startling development of the calmly
pretty valley of the Dee, along which we had
driven. Large, but by no means stupendous,
hills swelled prosperous and green on either side
of it, pine-woods thatched them warmly and
liberally, the Dee was irreproachably devious in
its advance and charming in its manners, but no
climax was arrived at, nor yet was contrast lying

in wait. If the poets had spared it their fine speeches, and their compliments fledged with suave metre, Llangollen could be appraised with a fresher eye and admired to the utmost of its mild deserving without antagonism and without disappointment. Also, if it is seen on the way into Wales instead of on the way out of it, it will occupy with fitting distinction its place in the crescendo of Welsh scenery, undiscounted by the coming fortissimo : to be one of the last notes in a diminuendo is quite a different thing.

Probably it was the two unparalleled persons known as the Ladies of Llangollen who did most for its fame. They ran away from their Irish homes to go and live there, which in itself, from our point of view, suggests eccentricity. Perhaps it was in lifelong penance for this act that ever after they wore riding-habits, summer and winter, indoors and out. After a fortnight spent in riding-habits we could appreciate such an expiation, even though the equipment we had dedicated to the Tommies did not include powdered hair and cart-

wheel felt hats. Pardonable curiosity might well
have caused any traveller by the Holyhead coach
who could scrape up an introduction to climb the
hill to Plas Newydd ; but it was not upon curiosity alone that the ladies relied for society. They
had the agreeability that could at will turn the
sightseer into an acquaintance, the means to weld
with good dinners such acquaintanceships into
permanence ; and æsthetic taste, the best part of
a century ahead of their time, that taught them
to frame the grotesque romance of their lives
and appearance in antique and splendid surroundings—the leisurely collection of many years—till
the poets and other people of distinction turned,
somewhat dazed, from the marvels of silver and
brass and carved oak, and, looking over the pleasant vale of Llangollen from windows set deep in
wood-carving, pronounced it to be unique.

The sun was very hot that afternoon as we
climbed on foot the steep hill up to Plas Newydd,
and it was difficult to receive with *sangfroid*, either
moral or physical, the intelligence that visitors

were not admitted on Sunday.   All that remained
was to sit exhausted on the grass, and stare with
amazement at the lacework of black carved wood
spread upon the white walls.   Not a nook without
a satyr head or a writhing animal, not a doorway
without its bossy pent-house, not a window without its special pattern of lattice panes, each repre-
senting a special acquisition, and doubtless a vast
wear and tear of riding - habit.   Their work is
respected, and the plain two-storey house still
holds like a casket the treasures of their finding,
and stands, crusted with ornament, as freshly
white and black as when the ladies took tea in
their porch with Wordsworth or Sir Walter Scott.
We hung about the small pleasure-grounds for
a little, among antique stone fonts and sundials,
and tried to find it pleasant ; but the exasperation
induced by a narrow vision of strange and lovely
things, half seen through a lancet-window, would
not be denied, and we presently went sulkily back
to the Grapes Hotel.   The Arch-Druid was awaiting us : we saw from afar his white beard, throned

high in the governess-cart, and felt its reproof and
suitability for pulpit denunciation; his cough as-
serted his wrongs indignantly outside, during an
otherwise unalloyed tea in the Grapes drawing-
room; and his thoughts were, it was easy to
suppose, back in the brave old Druidic days,
when he would have driven forth to meet the
tourist with scythes shining on the splinter-bar
of the governess-cart, and discouraged his vicious
trifling by utilising him as a burnt-offering.

He found, however, a poor nineteenth-century
revenge in obliging the black mare to consume,
at our expense, three feeds of corn. Such, at
least, was the astonishing item in the bill; and,
in a temporary lapse from the austerity of the
sacerdotal mood, he stooped to a refection that
called itself tea, and, judging by its price, must
have been of considerable extent.

CHAPTER XII.

WITH the alien literature of the Visitors' Book,
Wales is endowed beyond all countries known to
us. Here, more than elsewhere, does the Bir-
mingham tourist, hitherto mute and inglorious,
become sensible of inspiration, and enter deliri-
ously into poesy; here the funny man scintillates
with inveterate brilliancy, and the conscientious
churn forth adulation of scenery or cook, with
solemn and almost death-bed conviction.

The funny man is, as might be expected, widely
prevalent—he is, indeed, inexhaustible; and having
achieved immortality by his own personal entry,
gambols at large through the thumbed pages, and
bestows it upon the signatures of the less gifted
by lavish and sparkling comment. We find him

figuring as "Claud Hugo on the booze." "T'other
man playing the giddy bug." Or as "Mr and Mrs
Augustus Thompson on *treaclemoon.*" We cannot
lay claim to the italics ; they emanate from the
funny man, and partake of his inveteracy. We
traced him through Wales in a variety of titles,
almost classable as the Visitors' Book Peerage
—as, for instance, Lord Llanberis, Lord Shag,
Duke of Seven Dials, Lord Watkins, Earl of Bird,
Queen of Table Waters. He warned us, in an
eruption of notes of exclamation, to "beware of
potass and sodas in Wales," and was himself
eclipsed by an inspired commentator, who added
in pencil, "and every other ass."

The breezy and hardy athlete, also largely re-
presented, partakes of the nature of the funny
man, but has a liver unfitted for cynicism. He
is usually replete with the glory of his miles
per diem, and can only spare breath for a robust
epigram, such as "The breakfast we eat here this
morning will live in our remembrance." (Note by
funny man) "And the landlady's."

But it is to conscientious encomium that the Visitors' Book is indebted for its chiefest adornments and its most varied types, though of these it is possible only to cite the more salient. There is the encomium which, though conscientious towards the landlady, sets forth with an equal sense of justice the classical acquirements of the writer. It is a large class, but one example will suffice :—

"The Inn had in mind by he who wrote, 'shall I not take mine ease in mine inn?'"

There is the pathetic yet faithful encomium : "The above" (a list of names not as yet of historical interest), "during a week of hard and anxious literary work, felt quite at home here, thanks to the kindness of Mrs Jones and the untiring attention of Ellen in the coffee-room." Even the funny man has respected this tribute to female devotion — but in what did Ellen's attention consist? Did she, blending in her own person the hero-worship of Desdemona and the more solid abnegations of Molière's cook, sit as audience, even as critic, to the achievements

of that hard and anxious week? Or, accepting
the eulogy in a simpler sense, did she feed the
party hourly from an egg-spoon? We know that
she enhanced the home-like effect, and the rest
is silence.

The impassioned: "Lord keep my memory
green. — Wellesley Robinson." (First commentator) "Whoever is this fellow?" (Second do.)
"God knows."

The serious and almost religious :—

> "With plenty here the board is spread,
> And, e'er our onward path we tread,
> We feed from the' abundant store
> And sound it's praises more and more."

The influence of Tate and Brady is evident from
the mechanical addition of the apostrophe after
"the," which is reproduced in its integrity, in
common with all expression marks and feats of
English grammar throughout the collection.

The excessively gentle yet condescending:
"J. Brown. I am pleased with Cambria's lovely
vales."

M

The aristocratic but scarcely grammatical:
" Lord and Lady D—— for lunch. Very nice."

With these panegyrics we have not been moved
to compete. Not even the glistening dawn of
our last day in Wales prevailed, with its silent
greeting, to make us emulate J. Brown or Wellesley Robinson in their valedictory " appreciations."
In vows and protestations let us rather play
Cordelia to their Goneril and Regan, reserving
ourselves for that possible future when Wales,
repudiated of its Wellesley Robinsons, forsaken
as Lear, shall clamour for our support. Till then,
let the name of O'Flannigan and that other allied
with it, achieve in the Visitors' Book the distinction of beauty unadorned and verdict unvouch-
safed.

If the truth must be told, the dawn that
heralded our exit from Wales suggested little to
the eyes that turned away from it into the pro-
found sleep that heralds the hot water, and that
little was exclusively connected with horse-boxes.
Tommy the elder, though much recovered of the

girth-gall, was very far from being fit for a saddle, therefore the idea of a sensational finish on horse-back at the central lamp-post in Welshpool had been abandoned, and the Tommies were to be returned to the ironmonger and the chemist in the ordinary course of rail *via* Ruabon. We were sentimentally anxious to maintain as long as possible our auntly relation with them, even to the extent of travelling in the horse-box, and holding their hands and giving them sal volatile in the tunnels—this being, to the best of our belief, their first experience of travelling otherwise than on their own legs. The confidence inspired by human companionship would of course make everything easy; nevertheless, when at the station we saw their special carriage bear down upon us, behind an engine exuding steam at every pore and uttering yell upon yell as it came, it seemed possible that our nephews would require more than moral support. The engine steamed by, the doors of the horse-box were banged open, and we each took hold of a Tommy and prepared to lead

it as if it were a forlorn hope. Perhaps the ostlers
and porters whom we waved aside were not as
conscious as we presently became that the Tommies were more than willing to enter the box,
that they were hurrying up the clattering gangway, that they were almost ushering us into the
dark interior which we had regarded with such
sympathetic alarms. The porters and ostlers
laughed, but it may have been from pure admiration. The Corwen and Ruabon Railway seems
to be accustomed to the transportation of men-
ageries. Head - stalls that would have held a
buffalo were slipped upon the mildly aggrieved
pony faces, cables were attached to their nose-
bands on either side, and massive partitions were
let down between them. The Tommies were
obviously a little wounded, but beyond all other
emotions they were bored.

There are more luxurious places than the slice
that is stingily cut off the end of a horse-box
and apportioned to grooms. It is as third class
as a third class on the Cork and Skibbereen

Railway—that is to say, it has neither cushions nor blinds, and the brake and axle seem to dis-locate endless vertebræ in their anatomy immedi-ately under the seat; but it has attractions, even when shared with two side-saddles, each of which takes as much room as three women and a basket. There is sole and undisputed possession, and there is the tranquillity of those who look on junc-tions and are never shaken, when the horse-box moves majestic among the interwoven points to the appointed platform, whither the purple aristocracy of the first class must toil by stair-case and bridge. There are also two loopholes opening directly into the mangers of the horse-box, and through these, during the earlier part of the journey, we watched with concern the whites of the Tommies' eyes glistening in the obscurity as they glared in vast query upon us and all things; but beyond distended nostrils and immovably pricked ears they made no comment on the situation.

The valley of the Dee jogged past, in accord

with the bone - setting canter of the grooms'
carriage—a landscape always pretty, never startling, laden in the bright hot morning with the
trance of June, and with the tenderness of its
unconscious farewell to us. That one-sided fore-
knowledge of parting pervaded all things, and
indued with romance the two inquiring faces
—one bay with a white spot, the other drab with
a white blaze—that gazed at us across the empty
mangers in unwearied expectancy of oats. At
Ruabon Junction, during a long, hot interval in
a siding, we fed them with penny buns and with
an armful of hay stolen by Miss O'Flannigan
from a cart that stood outside a public - house
adjacent to our siding. It was an unusual manifestation of sentiment, but it was accepted on its
merits ; and the lumps of warm dough were chewed
and gulped with much fuss and detail, and the hay
snatched from our hands with a voracity that we
ventured to hope was a politeness. When, at
Oswestry, the final moment came, they suffered

A final salute.

with dignity the farewell endearments of their
aunts, staring through their loopholes with complete stolidity, after the manner of horse-flesh.
Their liquid brown eyes expressed nothing beyond a desire for more penny buns; and when
Miss O'Flannigan attempted, with a good deal
of personal effort, to imprint a final salute upon
her Tom's ruddy brown muzzle, he snorted with
apprehension and withdrew to the extremest
limits of his cable.   It was impossible to explain
to them that we found some difficulty in parting
with them, friends but of a fortnight though they
were.

And in parting, too, from the other features of
that fortnight,—from the leisure and indepen-
dence, the fatigue and inconvenience, the life ex-
panding unintellectually in long solitudes of open
sky, after shrivelling for three months in the
merely brain activity of London.   Travelling
towards Chester in the familiar monotony of a
railway carriage, the eye noted discontentedly the

level glide of the window along the landscape,
and endeavoured to catch at the quiet existence
of the country roads as the train took them at
a stride. The bounteous grave stillness of the
Welsh highways and mountain-fields was ours
no more ; that roomy calm, whose incidents were
a multiplication of peace, must intrench itself
in memory behind the dingy preoccupation of
catching a train at Chester, the crush of ugly,
self-centred people, the *blasé* porters, the importunities of little boys with cups of strong tea.

The climax of a variety of shocks to the rural
mood was reached at Holyhead with the discovery that our luggage, sent from Bettwys by
goods train, was not awaiting us. Whether or not
to start without it was a matter of poignant uncer-
tainty, even of frenzy, up to the moment when
the gangway of the Kingstown boat was hauled
in ; while the officials did not conceal their amuse-
ment, and the porter of the Station Hotel waited
immovable, in his red coat, foreknowing the end.

We stayed, and the Kingstown boat moved
out on an oily sea into a murky west, and the
rain began to fall.

www.ingramcontent.com/pod-product-compliance
Lightning Source LLC
Chambersburg PA
CBHW030558040726
47497CB00008B/2780